Louis Blois, John Duke Coleridge

A Mirror For Monks

Louis Blois, John Duke Coleridge

A Mirror For Monks

ISBN/EAN: 9783741183720

Manufactured in Europe, USA, Canada, Australia, Japa

Cover: Foto ©Andreas Hilbeck / pixelio.de

Manufactured and distributed by brebook publishing software
(www.brebook.com)

Louis Blois, John Duke Coleridge

A Mirror For Monks

A

MIRROR FOR MONKS.

WRITTEN BY

(LEWIS BLOSIUS,)

Louis de Blois

ABBOT OF ST. BENET'S ORDER.

EDITED, WITH A PREFACE, BY

SIR JOHN DUKE COLERIDGE,

HER MAJESTY'S ATTORNEY GENERAL,

M.P. FOR EXETER, AND LATE FELLOW OF EXETER COLLEGE, OXFORD.

LONDON:

C. J. STEWART, 11, KING WILLIAM STREET, W.C

1872.

PREFACE.

THE author of the following treatise, Louis
François de Blois, or (to adopt the style by
which, from the fact of his having written in
Latin, he is more commonly known) Ludovicus
Franciscus Blosius, was born in the month of
October, 1506, at the Chateau of Doustienne,
in the diocese of Liege, in Hainault. He was
of a house noble in itself, and connected with
more than one royal family, his father being
Adrian de Blois, Seigneur of Juvigni, and his
mother, Catharine de Barbançon. His parents
had ten children, six sons, most of them men
of distinction in their various ways of life, and
four daughters. The youngest daughter, under
the influence of her brother Louis, to whom
she was tenderly attached, devoted herself to
a Religious life, pursuing it with a gentle perseverance, of which the biographer of her
brother has left us a striking record. Blosius

was educated at the Court of Prince Charles, afterwards the Emperor Charles V., by whom he was greatly beloved, and who is said to have been a constant student of his writings. At the early age of fourteen he entered the Benedictine Order at the Monastery of Liessies, in Hainault, and in the course of a very few years the singular beauty of his character and the holiness of his life recommended him to the Abbot, Giles Gipius, as Coadjutor in the government of the Society. In 1530, while only twenty-four years old, he succeeded Giles as Abbot. From that time till his death in 1563 or 1566 (the date of his death appears to be uncertain), he devoted himself entirely to the government of his monastery, to the improvement of its discipline, and the ripening and strengthening of its Religious character, both by his own personal influence and example, and by a new body of statutes which he drew up, and for which he procured the approval of Pope Paul III. in 1545. The Abbacy of Tournay and the Archbishopric of Cambray were pressed upon him in vain by Charles V. He would not leave his monastery, and lived and died an example of that holy life which it is the main object of all his works to build up and confirm in others.

His works fill a folio volume, are written in Latin, and are entirely devotional. The most famous of them is the little treatise, an old translation of which is now reprinted. It was published by Blosius under the assumed name of the Abbot Dacryanus, and during his life-time he never openly acknowledged himself its author. Indeed, in the Life of Blosius prefixed to the complete edition of his works, published at Ingoldstadt in 1726, under the care of Anthony de Winghe, there is an elaborate discussion whether it was in truth the work of Dacryanus or of Blosius himself. There can be no kind of doubt, however, that Blosius wrote it. There never was an Abbot Dacryanus, and the name itself, the "Weeper," is manifestly symbolical of the contents of the book.

The MIRROR FOR MONKS has been very popular. It has been translated into French, first by De la Nauze, in 1726, and secondly by the celebrated De Lamennais, in 1820. De Lamennais prefixed to his edition a striking Preface, eulogizing ascetic writers in general, and Blosius in particular. "It would be a great mistake," says he, "to suppose, on account of this title, that it is of use only to those for whom it seems to have been principally composed. There is no Christian, in whatever station he may be, who may not read it and meditate upon it with profit. All the precepts of the spiritual life, all the counsels which can lead to perfection, are here brought together, and we are not afraid to say, presented with a charm of manner which renders them attractive, without any touch of the scholastic dryness which too often mars the best works of this kind. We know none, not even excepting the *Imitation of Christ*, so superior in other respects, which unites in the same degree sweetness, tenderness, lively feeling, and naïve expression. One sees and feels throughout that the author is himself penetrated by the truths he proclaims, for 'the heart of the wise teacheth his mouth, and addeth learning to his lips.'"*

The English translation here reprinted was published in Paris in 1676, and has become now a book of extreme rarity. The copy used for this reprint, the use of which I owe to the kindness of Mr. Richmond, is, in spite of many endeavours to procure another, the only one I ever saw. The book is not mentioned in the last edition of Brunet, and only one example of it is noticed in Mr. Bohn's edition of Lowndes.

I have made the spelling conform to our present usage. The spelling of 1676, at any rate the spelling of this book, has no philological value. It is simply bad and incorrect spelling; and to have retained it would have been valueless to the scholar, and a mere hindrance to the free use of the work itself as a book of devotion or meditation.

* Proverbs xvi. 23.

I am unable to give any account of the translation, or to say who was the translator. There are a considerable number of like translations, of more or less merit, made about the same time, and published abroad for the use of English Roman Catholics living in foreign countries. The writers of these books never returned to England; the readers of them were gradually merged into the population of the foreign countries where they lived; and thus the history of the books, and the very names of their writers, are now unknown, at least in England, and possibly have perished altogether.

I, at any rate, can furnish no information : but I hope the beauty and value of the book itself will be a sufficient reason for its being reprinted with any one who reads it. I have no other reason to give for reprinting it, but that I hope it may do good. Blosius, it is true, was a Roman Catholic Abbot of the sixteenth century. But it may soften prejudice and enlarge sympathy to find, as in the much higher example of the *Imitation of Christ,* how pure, how simple, how Scriptural, how devout, how intensely and essentially Christian was the religion taught and practised by such a man at such a time. I might indeed, as both the French translators did, have softened the title, which as it stands may awaken prejudice; and have altered a sentence here and there, with which, perhaps, all readers belonging to the Church of England may not agree. But I have thought it best to leave Blosius as I found him, and as his English translator left him. The MIRROR FOR MONKS is really a looking-glass for Christians, and to Christian readers I commend it.

JOHN DUKE COLERIDGE.

Buckland Court, Ashburton,
    1st October, 1870.

———————

I had intended to confine the reprint of this translation to the very limited number of copies which during the present year have been placed in the hands of those few persons I thought might feel interested in the matter. But the little book has excited more interest and been received with more favour than I expected; and I have been advised by some, to whose opinion and wishes I owe every deference, to allow of its publication Among these I may mention Dr. Newman, Mr. Gladstone, and my father, Sir John Taylor Coleridge. Accordingly the book is now published, contrary to my original intention, but no doubt on my responsibility.

It is hardly necessary to say that I do not agree with every theological doctrine which Blosius assumes or inculcates in his book. But I think the book in itself a good and beautiful book; I believe the writer of it to have been a holy man; and I do not think it right, in spite of high authority to the contrary, to mutilate or adapt such works as these. To do so appears to me unmanly and unfair. It is as if we were afraid of the soundness of our convictions, and dared not look in the face the fact that good men in other times did not share them. Whereas it is part of Christian history that very good and saintly men have held opinions in religion which we now think mistaken; and it is a narrow and shallow judgement which holds such opinions to be inconsistent with true and vital Christianity. This book, to my mind, proves that they are nowise inconsistent; and I most earnestly hope that those who read it carefully will think so too; and may find it kindle or increase in their hearts the love of God and of His Son.

JOHN DUKE COLERIDGE.

Buckland Court, Ashburton,
31st August, 1871.

A TABLE OF THE THINGS CONTAINED IN THIS TREATISE.

A MIRROR FOR MONKS.

—•—

CHAPTER I.

YOU desire of me, beloved Brother Odo, a spiritual mirror or looking-glass, wherein you may behold yourself, and exactly see both your beauty and deformity. This request of yours is somewhat strange. Certainly, I think that you know me not; for if you did, whence doth it happen, that you request a spiritual thing of a carnal man? Nevertheless, lest I might seem to neglect, or rather to contemn your request, behold I send what our penury hath been able to afford you. Accept therefore of this short instruction, by reading whereof you may peradventure slenderly learn what you are, what you are not, or certainly what you ought to be.

First and foremost, therefore, I admonish you often and seriously to consider the end of your

B

coming into your monastery; that being dead to
the world and yourself, you may live to God.
Strive therefore with might and main to accomplish
that for which you came; learn strongly to despise
all sensible things, and manfully to break, and no
less wholesomely to forsake yourself. Make haste
to mortify your passions and vicious affections that
are in you.

Busy yourself in repressing the unstable wanderings of your heart; strive to overcome weariness,
idleness, and the irksomeness of your infirm mind.
Spend your daily labour in these things; let this
be your glorious contention and healthful affliction.
Be not remiss; but arise, watch, look about you,
and expose yourself wholly, lest you be evilly
partial to yourself. God requireth thus much of
you; so doth your state.

You are called a Monk: see that you be truly
what you are called. Do the work of a Monk.
Labour earnestly in beating down and casting forth
vice.

Be always armed against the frowardness of
nature, against the haughtiness of mind, against
the pleasures of your flesh, and the enticements of

sensuality. Understand well what I say. If you permit pride, boasting, vainglory, self-complacence, to domineer over your reason, you are no Monk.

If you frowardly follow your own sense, and dare despise every humble office, you are not what you are called—you are no Monk.

If as much as in you lieth you repel not envy, hatred, maliciousness, indignation; if you reject not rash suspicions, childish complaints, and wicked murmurings, you are no Monk.

If a contentious and earnest strife being risen between you and another, you do not presently treat of a reconciliation, and what wrong soever hath been done, you do not presently pardon sincerely, but seek for revenge, and retain a voluntary private grudge, and not a true and sincere affection in your heart, or show outwardly signs of disaffection—nay, if when occasion and necessity requireth, you defer to help him that hath injured you, you are no Monk, you are no Christian, you are abominable before God.

If having done amiss, you are ashamed regularly to accuse yourself and freely to confess your fault; if being blamed, reproved, and corrected, you be not patient and humble, you are no Monk.

If you neglect readily and faithfully to obey your ghostly Father, if you refuse to reverence and sincerely to love him as God's vicar, you are no Monk.

If you willingly withdraw yourself from the Divine Office and other conventual acts, if you assist not watchfully and reverently in the service of God, you are no Monk.

If, neglecting internal things, you take care only about the external, and with a certain dry custom move your body but not your heart to the works of religion, you are no Monk.

If you give not your mind to holy reading and other spiritual exercises, if you have your mind so possessed with transitory matters that you seldom lift yourself up to eternal, you are no Monk.

If you desire delicate and superfluous meats, and intemperately long after the drinking of wine beyond the measure of a cup, especially if you be in health, and have beer or other convenient drink sufficiently, you are no Monk.

If foolishly you require precious apparel, soft beds, and other solaces of the flesh which agree not with your state and profession ; if, loving corporal rest, you refuse to undergo labour and affliction for God's sake, you are no Monk.

If you cannot endure solitude and silence, but are delighted with idle speeches and inordinate laughter, you are no Monk.

If you love to be with seculars, if you desire to wander out of the monastery through the villages and cities, you are no Monk.

If you presume to take any small matter, to send, receive, or keep any things without the knowledge or permission of your Superior, you are no Monk.

If you esteem not the ordinations of holy religion, though never so little, and willingly do transgress them, you are no Monk. To conclude : If you seek any other thing in the monastery but God, and with might and main aspire not to perfection, you are no Monk.

As I have said, therefore, that you may truly be what you are called, and may not wear the habit of a Monk in vain, do the work of a Monk.

Arm yourself against yourself, and as much as in you lieth overcome and subdue yourself. If presently you find not the peace you desire; if, I say, as yet you cannot be at rest, but are troubled and assailed by brutish motions and turbulent passions : yea, if so be by God's permission, for your own profit, throughout your whole life you shall have to do with such enemies, despair not, be not effeminately dejected, but, humbling yourself before God, stand and be steadfast in your place, and skirmish stoutly ; for even the vessel of election, St. Paul, endured temptations all his life-time, in which he was buffeted by the angel of Satan. When he often beseeched our Lord to be freed from this trouble he obtained it not, for that it was not expedient for him ; but our Lord answered his prayer, "My grace is sufficient for thee, for strength is perfected in weakness." And so afterwards St. Paul did gratefully endure the scourge of temptation. Being comforted by the example of this most strong and invincible champion, faint not in temptation, but endure manfully, remaining fixed and immoveable in this holy purpose ; for without doubt, this labour of yours is grateful to God, although the same seem hard and insufferable to you. Go through this spiritual martyrdom with an invincible mind. Doubt not, although you be a thousand times wounded, and as often trod under foot, if you stand to it, if you give not ground to your enemy and like a coward cast not away your weapons, you shall receive a crown. Do according to your ability, and commend the rest to God's disposing, saying: As Thy will is in Heaven, so be it done. Let the divine will and ordination be your chief consolation. Which way soever you turn yourself, wheresoever you are, you shall find tribulations and temptations as long as this life lasteth; which, that you may patiently endure, you ought always to be prepared.

But you are happy, if by grace you have proceeded so far that all grief and affliction whatsoever become truly pleasing to you for God's sake. What think you, Brother, is my glass big enough; or is not this yet sufficient for you, but you yet desire to hear in more express terms, more abundantly and fully, how to compose yourself within and without, or how, according to reason, you ought to order every day before God.

CHAPTER II.

As soon as you are awake and ready to rise to
Matins, devoutly arm yourself with the sign of
the Cross, and briefly pray to God that He will
vouchsafe to blot out the stains of sin in you,
and be pleased to help you. Then, casting all
vain imaginations out of your mind, think upon
some other thing that is spiritual, and conceive as
much purity of heart as you can, rejoicing in yourself that you are called up to the praise and
worship of your Creator. But if frailty of body,
if heaviness of sleep, if conturbation of spirit,
depress you, be not out of heart, but be comforted
and force yourself, overcoming all impediments
with reason and willingness ; for the Kingdom of
Heaven suffereth violence, and the violent take it
by force. Certainly, according to the labour which

you undergo for the love of God, such shall be your recompense and reward. Being come off from your bed, commend and offer yourself, both body and soul, to the Most High ; make haste to the choir, as to a place of refuge and the garden of spiritual delights. Until Divine Office begins, study to keep your mind in peace and simplicity, free from troubles and the multiplicity of uncertain thoughts ; collecting a goodly and sweet affection towards your God by sincere meditation or prayer. In the performance of the Divine Office have a care to pronounce and hear the holy words reverently, perfectly, thankfully, and attentively, that you may taste that your Lord is sweet, and may feel that the Word of God hath incomprehensible sweetness and power. For whatsoever the Holy Ghost hath dictated is indeed the life-procuring food, and the delightful solace of a chaste, sober, and humble soul. Remember, therefore, to be there faithfully attentive, but avoid too vehement cogitations and motions of mind ; especially if your head be weak, lest being hurt or wearied, confounded and straitened internally, you shut the sanctuary of God against yourself. Reject, likewise, too troublesome care, which commonly bringeth with it pusillanimity and restlessness, and persevere with a gentle, quiet, and watchful spirit in the praises of God, without singularity. But if you cannot keep your heart from wanderings, be not dejected in mind; but patiently endeavour, patiently do what lieth in your power, committing the rest to the divine will. Persevere in your goodly affection towards God, and even your very defects, which you are no way able to exclude, will in a manner beget you consolation. For as the earth, which is of a convenient nature, doth by the casting of dung, oftentimes more faithfully send forth her seeds; so a mind of goodwill, out of the defects which by constraint it sustaineth, shall in due time receive the most sweet fruit of divine visitation, if it endure them with patience.

And what profit do you reap by being impatient? Do you not heap calamity upon calamity? Do you not show your want of true humility, and bewray in yourself a pernicious propriety?*

---

* This word is here used in a sense perhaps new to many readers. It does not of course mean what we now commonly understand by it ; but is used by Blosius and by many other ascetic writers to signify

As long as you do reverently assist, and are ready with a prompt desire of will to attend, you have satisfied God; neither will He impute the inordinateness of this instability to you, if so be by your negligence you give not consent unto it, and before the time of prayer you set a guard over your senses. If you cannot offer a perfect dutifulness, offer at least a good will: offer a right intent in the spirit of humility; and so the devil shall not find any occasion to cavil against you. Although you have nothing else to offer but a readiness, in body and spirit, to serve our Lord in holy fear, be sure of it that you shall not lose your reward. But, woe to your soul, if you be negligent and remiss, and care not to give attendance; for it is written—"Cursed is the man that doth the work of God negligently." Be diligent, that you may perform what you are able, if you

---

a habit of mind the opposite of that which is expressed by the word "detachment." "Self-seeking" has been suggested to me as an equivalent, but it hardly is so. Perhaps "the thinking of things solely with reference to oneself," or "a desire to possess things whether temporal or spiritual for oneself alone," would express the idea intended to be conveyed by the word. But the periphrasis would be long and awkward, and I leave the word as it is, here and elsewhere in the treatise, with this explanation.

be not able to perform what you desire. Upon this security, be not troubled when impediments happen, and you be not able to perform as much as you would. When, I say, distraction of your senses, dejection of mind, dryness of heart, grief of head, or any other misery or temptation afflicteth you, beware you say not : I am left, our Lord hath cast me away, my duty pleaseth Him not. These are words befitting the children of distrust. Endure, therefore, with a patient and joyful mind all things for His sake that hath called and chosen you, firmly believing that He is near to those that are of a contrite heart. For if you humbly, without murmuring, carry this burden laid on you, not by mortal tongue to be uttered, what a deal of glory you heap up for yourself in the life to come. You may truly say unto God : As a beast am I become with Thee. Believe me, Brother, if being replete with internal sweetness, and lifted up above yourself, you fly up to the third heaven, and there converse with Angels, you shall not do so great a deed as if for God's sake you shall effectually endure grief and banishment of heart and be conformable to our Saviour; when, in extreme sorrow, anguish, fear, and adversity, crying unto His Father—"Let Thy will be done;" Who also, being thrust through His hands and feet, hanging on the Cross, had not whereon to lean His Head; Who also most lovingly endured for thee all the griefs and disgraces of His most bitter Passion. Therefore, in holy longanimity, contain yourself, and expect in silence until it shall please the Most High to dispose otherwise. And certainly in that day it shall not be demanded of you how much internal sweetness you have here felt; but how faithful you have been in the love and service of God.

CHAPTER III.

GOD HATH TWO SORTS OF SERVANTS, AND THE DESCRIPTION OF BOTH.

AMONG those that are called the servants of God, many serve Him unfaithfully, few faithfully. Indeed, unfaithful servants, as long as they have sensible devotion and present grace of tears, do serve God with alacrity, they pray willingly, joyfully go about good works, and seem to live in deep peace of heart; but as soon as God hath thought it good to withdraw that devotion, you shall see them troubled, chafe, become malicious and impatient, and at last neither willing to be at their prayers nor any other divine exercises. And because they feel not internal consolations as they desire, they perniciously betake themselves to those that are external and contrary to the spirit, whereby it is manifest that they are not purely God's gift, and abuse them to their own pleasure; for if they did love God purely, and did not viciously rest in

His gifts, they would remain peaceable in God, those gifts being taken away; and would not even then turn out of the way to unlawful consolations. Therefore they are unfaithful, because in adversity they keep not touch with God. They believe for awhile, and shrink back in time of trial. They would have all things go on their side, and endure nothing that goeth against them. If God grant those things that they would have, they serve Him; if He deny them, they leave Him—nay, in prosperity they serve not God, but themselves; and in all things would rather have their own will done than God's. They place sanctity in internal sweetness and consolation, rather than in the perfect mortification of vices; being ignorant that by the withdrawing of devotion it more certainly appeareth, if one truly love God, than by the infusion of it. For that sensible devotion is commonly more truly a natural than spiritual devotion.

But whatsoever it be, unless a man make use of it wisely, it is wont oftentimes to bring him that is so affected to a hidden kind of pride, a wicked complacence and a vain security, as we daily see in these unfaithful servants. For as soon

as they are tickled with this inward sweetness, they
will forsooth begin to judge and despise others:
they think themselves great saints, and the secre-
taries of God; they expect and wonderfully long
after divine revelations, and wish that some miracles
were done by them, or of them, by which others
might take notice of the holiness which they think
they have, but have not. Thus do they use to
vanish away in their own imaginations, who gape
more after sensible grace than the Giver of grace.
But faithful servants behave themselves far otherwise, for they seek not themselves, but God;
neither their own consolation, but chiefly the will
and honour of God; they always fly propriety;
whether God be pleased to infuse or not to infuse
the influence of internal sweetness, they are all
one, and persisting in equality of mind cease not
to love and praise God. It is not internal darkness,
nor difficulty of senses, nor coldness of affections,
nor dryness of heart, nor dejection of mind, nor
drowsiness of spirit, nor adversity of temptation;
to conclude, it is neither misery of adversity, nor
success of prosperity, that is able to heave them
out of their place; for although, peradventure, they

feel in the inferior powers of the soul the oppression of inordinate sorrow proceeding from adversity, or the violence of sensual delight arising out of prosperity, they are not for all that dejected, because they continue quiet in the reason or higher part of the soul, and do conform their will to the divine will or permission, and grieve that they feel the least contradiction of unseemly motions. Being founded, therefore, as a firm rock, they persist steadfast in the love of God, as they whose chief comfort is in His will. They are always devout, because with all their power they avoid and abhor whatsoever is displeasing to God, and may never so little contaminate the purity of their heart; and, committing themselves in all chances to God, do still possess a pure, free, and quiet mind. This is the truest devotion and most acceptable to God. The other sensible devotion, which is more familiar to novices, or those that are lately converted, is not durable and sure, yet notwithstanding it is very profitable to us if we wisely make use of it. The faithful servants (for so I still call them, whom Christ calleth not servants, but friends), faithful servants, I say, do seek after that effectual

C

and most pleasant sweetness of grace also; they
seek after the joy of our Lord's salvations; they
seek after His most lovely countenance and most
sweet embraces, but they do this with a spiritual
and bashful, not with a sensual, greediness, or
childish lightness, or a troubled impatience. They
desire the gifts of God, not that they may be sensually delighted in them, but that, being made more
fervent by them, and more pure from all inordinateness, they may please their heavenly Bridegroom.
They love the gifts of God, and willingly thank
Him for them; but yet they keep themselves, as
it were, quiet and free from them as long as they
rest not in them. By grace they go forward to
the Giver of Grace and Supreme Good, in Whom
only it is lawful for them to rest. They are truly
happy, because by how much the less they stick
to those gifts they receive so many the more.

And although they be never so much endowed
with blessings from God, they lift not up their
mind, they despise not others, but themselves; I
say, they despise and acknowledge themselves
unworthy of all spiritual grace, they always keep
in mind that whatsoever they have it is of God's

mere mercy, and that of them more is exacted to whom more is given or committed. And so continuing in holy fear, and by these gifts proceeding in humility, they confess themselves to be below the lowest. They rejoice and glory within themselves if, being oppressed with unjust infamy, reproaches, injuries, and uttermost scorn, they have imitated Christ; not if they could be elevated above themselves by excess of mind, or could see strange visions, or do most apparent miracles. They, presently making the sign of the Cross, repel the deceitful suggestions by which the devil endeavours to allure them to vainglory and self-complacence, no way consenting to the subtleties of the wicked serpent. They do not confidently place the loss of their salvation either in the number or in the merit of good works which they do, but put their trust in the freedom of the sons of God, which they have obtained by the blood of Christ. We then, brother, knowing the difference of the faithful servants, endeavour to be of those which, may be, you are not of, and strive to leave them of whom, peradventure, you are one. If you are of those you would not be of, and are

C 2

not of those of whom you would be, grieve and
humble yourself, for God giveth grace to the humble.
And certainly, if you humble yourself in the sight
of our Lord, grieving that you are yet of the number
of the unfaithful, you have already in a manner
passed into the lot of the faithful ; 'labour, persevere,
fear not. You shall not be reproved with the
unfaithful, but shall be received with the faithful.

There are others also that are bound to the
divine service, and yet cannot be called either
faithful or unfaithful servants of God ; these a
man may lawfully call the idle slaves of the devil.
I mean those unhappy wretches that, esteeming
either not at all, or very little, of devotion or the
grace of God, and altogether neglecting the interior
parts, make a show, as though they honoured God
with their lips, but their heart is far from Him.
These being plunged over head and ears in a sea
of evil, do little think of their own salvation.
These are all one to-day as they were yesterday.
They came from the choir as they went thither,
viz., unclean, tepid, apt to no goodness, wandering, dissolute, without fear, without reverence. By
the divine praises, which with a polluted mouth they

utter, they more exasperate than please. I would
to God these had kept them in the world ; for what
do they in monasteries? why tread they on holy
ground? why devour they the alms of the just?
why pollute they the angelical schools of spiritual
exercises with carnal delights? If they intended
to live uncleanly, they should have remained in
a place for their purpose, and not have entered into
places of purity. Living negligently in monasteries,
they double the punishments of hell which their
ill living in the world had deserved. But it is out
of our way to speak more of these things ; wherefore I return whence I strayed.

CHAPTER IV.

THAT FOR EVERY HOUR OF THE DAY WE OUGHT TO CLEAVE TO SOME SETTLED EXERCISE, LEST OUR MIND GROW SLUGGISH.

So that you may be settled in your private exercise, prescribe yourself something what to do every hour, and to be busied in. But so that, if at any time, either upon obedience or any other private reasonable cause or chance happening, you abbreviate your exercise or wholly overslip it, you be not inordinately vexed, for you ought chiefly to endeavour to attain to this, that in the liberty and purity of heart (rejecting all propriety) you may always persevere, peaceable and without trouble before God. For this is acceptable to our Lord above all other exercises, be they never so laborious and hard. Whatsoever, therefore, shall hinder this liberty in you, although it be spiritual and seem very profitable, occasion so requiring, leave it as much as obedience doth permit. Endeavour, I say, to repel all restless-ness of heart, which choketh true peace and perfect trust in God with all spiritual proceedings. Let not vicious idleness at any time take place, for it destroyeth souls. Avoid also idle businesses; I mean those that are unprofitable, neither marvel at this kind of speech. Let not vicious idleness at any time take place, for there is also a commendable idleness, which is when the soul, fixed on God, and exempted from the noise and imagination of all sensible things, doth rest as it were idle in internal silence, and in the most blessed embracements of her Beloved, to which, if the hand of our Lord bring you, you shall profitably and happily be idle. Otherwise, always either read, or meditate, or pray, or take in hand something else that shall be serious and necessary; and truly, if you will settle yourself with all diligence to the study of Scripture you will be wonderfully comforted, and every spiritual thing will begin to grow sweet unto you, and so it will come to pass that, being accustomed to holy delights, you will easily condemn those that are carnal, and your mind will be wonderfully strengthened in your good purpose. To the end, therefore, that you may merit so great a fruit, willingly and wisely give yourself to reading; that is to say, in reading seek spiritual consolation and profit and the love of God, not curiosity, not superfluous understanding and knowledge, not neatness and elegance of words; for the Kingdom of God is not in elegance of speech but in holiness of life, which elegance of speech, nevertheless, as it is not over-carefully to be sought after if it be wanting, so it is not scornfully to be rejected by him that hath it, for it is also the gift of God. Receive all things with thanksgiving, and all things shall help forward for your salvation. Howbeit, be not troubled if many of those good things which you hear or read slip out of your memory. For as a vessel which often receiveth water remaineth clean, although the water poured in be presently poured out again, so likewise, if spiritual doctrine often run through a well-willing mind, although it abide not there, nevertheless it maketh and keepeth the mind clean and pleasing to God. Your chief profit consisteth, not in committing the word of doctrine to memory, but rather that the effects of the doctrine and words remain in you, that is by this doctrine to get an internal purity, and a ready mind to fulfil the commandments of God. Learn to apply those things to yourself that are spoken against vice, for it is not safe to assert them against others with a fixed judgement of mind, lest while you obstinately judge another you defile or trouble your own conscience. And so, in all things which seem any way obscene, avoid as much as in you lieth even the very least allurement of any slippery motion; if by way of temptation they do impugn, molest, and trouble you importunately, contradict them with reason, deny to give consent, and, making the sign of the Cross, direct your whole intention to God. For so without hurt you may escape this danger. Furthermore, do not imitate those that observe no order in reading, but do read what cometh first to hand and where they first open the book; they like nothing which is not new and strange, for they loathe all things that are usual and stale, though never so profitable. Far be such instability from you, for it doth not recollect but distract the spirit, and he is dangerously sick that is tainted with this disease. Wisely bind your mind to a certainty of reading, and accustom yourself to go through with it, although sometimes it administer no matter of pleasure.

Read, I say, not confusedly or disorderly, but methodically. Repeat those things again and again that are good. Nevertheless, in time of tribulation and spiritual poverty you may intermit what you have begun, and, according to your necessity, turn and apply yourself to other godly exercises which may be more consolatory.

For it is the opinion of the Fathers that it is good to go to prayer or meditation from reading, and again to have recourse to reading from prayer ; that prayer with a commendable vicissitude succeeding reading and reading succeeding prayer, loathsomeness may be taken away ; and the mind being, as it were, fresh and lusty, may always be the more able for the proposed work, and that the greater fruit may be reaped of both. And what hindrance is there why a man should not make short prayers even in reading, and aspire to God by holy desires ? There are many things that may serve either for reading or prayer or meditation : such are all the Scriptures in which there is conference with God. Always prefer common prayers before

private, and judge them to be more profitable for
you, although sometimes they may seem more
barren and unsavoury. In like manner, esteem of
all common and regular actions, for above all things
obedience ought to be in the first place. If,
peradventure, you demand in what prayers and
meditations you should in private chiefly exercise
yourself: if you will credit me, after you have
accused yourself and craved pardon for your sins,
you shall chiefly beseech God to mortify your evil
passions and vicious affections, and quite and clean
to strip you of all inordinateness ; and that He will
be pleased to grant you grace joyfully and patiently
to endure all tribulation and temptation. Ask of
Him profound humility and most fervent charity.
Beseech Him to vouchsafe always to direct, teach,
illuminate, and protect you in all things. These
things, in my judgement, are most necessary for
you. And, indeed, they are most great and high,
neither can they otherwise be obtained than by
prayer. Persevere, therefore, continually knocking ;
and without doubt our Lord will at length open
unto you, and will give you as much bread as your
necessity shall require. But so you neglect not

willingly to give thanks for what you have received. For nothing displeaseth God more than forgetfulness and ingratitude for received benefits. And that you may the more willingly and sooner incline God's benignity unto you, pray attentively for the state of the whole Church, commending unto God all the Faithful, both alive and dead, and every reasonable creature. Will you further hear in what with profit you may exercise yourself. I will tell you: singing of psalms is profitable, the godly meditating on other parts of Scripture is profitable, the consideration of creatures compared to their Creator is profitable.

CHAPTER V.

HOW POWERFUL AND EFFICACIOUS THE REMEM-BRANCE OF CHRIST'S LIFE AND PASSION IS.

ALL prayers, singing of hymns, thanksgiving, and holy meditations are profitable. But by consent of all, the remembrance of Christ's Humanity, and especially of His most sacred Passion, is said to be most profitable and only necessary, and with justice. For it is the present extermination of passions and inordinate affections, a fit refuge in temptation and surest safeguard in dangers, a sweet refreshing in distress, a friendly rest from labour, a gentle repressing of distractions, the true door of sanctity, the only entry to contemplation, the sweet consolation of the soul, the unfailing flame of divine love, the salver of all adversities, the fountain of all virtues, from whence they flow to us: to conclude, the absolute example of all perfection, the haven, hope, trust, merit, and salvation

of all Christians. I knew a Monk, whose custom
was to propose to himself every day some part of
our Lord's Passion, as, for example, one day he
would set before his eyes Christ's being in the
Garden. And whithersoever he went that day,
wheresoever he chanced to be, if not troubled with
any other serious and necessary cogitation, whatsoever he did outwardly, he took a special care
to direct his internal eye to our Lord suffering
distresses in the Garden, and thus would he talk
with his soul: And my soul, behold thy God.
Behold, daughter, attend, see, and consider, most
dear! Behold thy God, behold thy Creator, behold
thy Father, behold thy Redeemer and Saviour!
behold thy refuge, behold thy defender and pro-
tector, behold thy hope, trust, strength, and health!
Behold thy sanctification, purity, and perfection!
behold thy help, merit, and reward! behold thy
tranquillity, consolation, and sweetness! Behold thy
joy, thy delights, and thy life! behold thy light,
thy crown, and thy glory! behold thy love and thy
desire! behold thy treasure and all thy good! behold
thy beginning and thy end! Whither art thou
scattered, thou wandering daughter? How long wilt

thou leave the light and love darkness? How long wilt thou forsake peace and involve thyself in troubles! Return, return, thou Sunamite, return! Daughter, return and recollect thyself, most dear! leave many things and embrace one—for one thing is necessary for thee. Abide with thy Lord; place thyself by thy God; go not from thy Master; sit in His shadow Whom thou lovest, that His fruit may be sweet to thy throat. It is good for thee to be here, daughter. For hither the enemy cannot make his approach; here are no snares, no dangers, no darkness. All things are here safe, all things calm. Reside here willingly, most dear. For here thou shalt be safe and free, thou shalt be merry and joyful. Here are roses, lilies, and violets; here flowers of all virtues do smell most pleasantly. Here thou shalt see a brightness sweetly enlightening all things with his rays. Here thou shalt find true consolation; here thou shalt find peace and rest. To conclude, here thou shalt find all good.

With such short sentences he would both sharply and sweetly spur forward his soul, and call her home when she was wandering abroad, and force her to apply herself to the chiefest good. Of

these little sentences he would take sometimes
more, sometimes fewer, sometimes only one, sometimes two, sometimes three, according to the fervour
of his devotion and the pleasure of the Holy Ghost ;
and he would oftentimes iterate and repeat them.
He would also force his soul to the remembrance
of those things which our Saviour did and suffered
for her in the Garden. In the meantime, one
while exciting her to the considerations of our
Saviour's unsearchable humility, mildness, patience,
most fervent and incomprehensible charity ; another
while to take compassion on our Lord of infinite
majesty, so humbled and afflicted, and then again
to thank Him for so great benefits and piety ;
another while to repay love with love, and anon
to ask pardon for her sins, and then to beg
this or that grace. He would often convert his
speech to these or the like affectionate or fervent
aspirations : And my soul, when wilt thou be
ready to follow the humility of thy Lord ? when
wilt thou imitate His mildness ? when shall the
example of His patience shine in thee ? when wilt
thou be better ? when wilt thou be free from
passions and vicious affections ? when shall evil be

destroyed in thee? when shall all inordinateness be blotted out in thee? when wilt thou peaceably and gently endure all tribulation and temptation? when wilt thou perfectly love thy God? when wilt thou intimately embrace Him? when wilt thou be wholly swallowed up in His love? when wilt thou be pure, simple, and reserved before Him? how long will it be ere thou be hindered no more from His most chaste embracings? and that thou were immaculate; and that thou didst fervently love thy God; and that thou didst inseparably cleave unto thy chiefest good. And then directing the eye of his heart to Heaven or to the depth of eternal light, he would frame these aspirations: And my soul, where is thy God? where is thy love? where is thy treasure? where is thy desire? where is thy total good? when shalt thou see Him? when shalt thou most happily enjoy Him? when shalt thou freely praise Him with all the citizens of Heaven? These and the like aspirations would he secretly speak either mentally or with his lips, taking sometimes more, sometimes fewer, according to the internal motions of the Holy Ghost. He would also often accuse his soul, that it was

D

too slow, sluggish, tepid, ungrateful, hard, insensible, and unhappy. Again he would comfort it, being dejected with pusillanimity or fear, and would encourage it with these or the like words: Despair not my soul; take comfort, daughter, and be confident, most dear. If thou hast sinned and art wounded, behold thy God! behold thy Physician is ready to cure thee. He is most courteous and most merciful, and therefore willing; He is omnipotent, and therefore can pardon thy sins in a moment. Peradventure thou art afraid because He is thy Judge? but take heart, for He that is thy Judge is also thine Advocate. He is thy Advocate to defend and excuse thee, doing penance; He is, therefore, also thy Judge to save, not to condemn thee, being humbled. His mercy is infinitely greater than thy iniquity either is or can be. Which words I say not that, persevering in evil, thou shouldst make thyself unworthy of His mercy; but that, being averted from evil, thou shouldst not despair of indulgence and forgiveness. Thy God is most gentle, most sweet; He is wholly amiable, wholly desirable, and wonderfully loveth all things which He hath created. When thou thinkest of

Him, or conceivest Him in thy memory, far be all imagination of terror, austerity, and bitterness from thee. When we say He is terrible, it is not in respect of Himself, but of those that abuse His patience and defer to do penance, whose most bitter and poisonous sins, as contrary to His most sweet and pure goodness, He repelleth and punisheth. Let not thine imperfections discourage thee too much; for thy God doth not despise thee because thou art imperfect and infirm, but loveth thee exceedingly because thou desirest and labourest to be more perfect. He will also help thee if thou persistest in thy good intention, and will make thee perfecter—yea, peradventure (which thou little hopest for), wholly fair and every way pleasing to Him.

Thus, and in innumerable other ways, would he friendly talk with his soul, and invite her by chaste speeches to the chaste love of her Beloved. He would also turn his speech to our Lord, and, aspiring to Him by holy love, would say: And good JESUS, pious Pastor, sweet Master, King of eternal glory, when shall I be immaculate and truly humble before Thee? when shall I truly despise

D 2

all sensible things for Thee, and when shall I
perfectly forsake myself? when shall I be stripped
of all propriety? For, unless there were propriety
in me, there would not be self-will in me : passions
and inordinate affections would have no place in
me. I should not seek myself in anything. Propriety only maketh the impediment and medium
between Thee and me ; propriety only doth hinder
Thee from me. When, therefore, shall I cast off all
propriety? When shall I freely resign myself to
Thy divine pleasure? When shall I serve thee with
a clean, quiet, simple, and calm mind? When shall
I perfectly love Thee in the arms of my soul? When
shall I love Thee with most fervent desire? When
shall all my tepidity and imperfection be swallowed
up by the immensity of Thy love? O my desire,
my treasure, O my total good, O my beginning and
end, O my God, O sweetness of my soul, O my
consolation, my life, my love! Oh, that my soul
might enjoy Thy most sweet embracings! Oh, that
it were indissolubly bound with Thy love ; would it
were perfectly united to Thee. For what is to me
in Heaven, and besides Thee what would I upon
earth, God of my heart, and God my portion for

ever? When shall the world be silent to me? When shall the impediments, troubles, and vicissitudes of this life cease to me? When shall my pilgrimage be ended? When shall my sojourning be consummated? When shall the miserable captivity of this banishment be dissolved? When shall the shadow of mortality decrease and the day of eternity draw near? When shall I lay down the burden of this body and see Thee? When shall I praise Thee as Thy Saints, without impediment, happily, and eternally? O my God, my love, my total good! He was often wont to use such aspirations, knowing that by the exercise of them the human spirit is more effectually united to the divine spirit, and that thereby man attaineth the sooner to the perfect mortification of himself. He had them ready everywhere; but if at any time he had more sufficient leisure, he would then (sitting as Mary Magdalen did) rejoice to linger more freely, and that more to the honour of God than to the inordinate pleasing of himself. He would not in the meantime omit, with a certain internal effusion of heart, by a sincere and sweet affection, to adore, bless, give thanks, and pray. Moreover, turning his speech to the Blessed Virgin, the Mother of God, as to a most merciful lady, and most liberal stewardess of heavenly treasures, he would redouble his pious complaints before her, and, with a holy importunity, extort a benediction. Another day he would set before himself how our Saviour, betrayed by Judas, was taken, and concerning this point he would iterate his foresaid exercises, and so would go through with the Passion in order, and having ended would begin again. And about that part of the Passion which did represent Christ hanging on the Cross, he did not employ himself in order and in his proper day, but every day at least briefly, if so be he thought it convenient, exciting his soul to the earnest contemplation of these things. On every solemnity of our Saviour or the Blessed Virgin he would (if he thought it good) propose to the eyes of his mind the representation of that Feast instead of part of our Lord's Passion, which otherwise was that day to be frequented, and would perform his internal exercises or friendly discourses with his soul, and about the work, cause, mystery, and joy of that festivity. He was also much delighted with singing the Psalms. And I know that, by the continued custom of this holy exercise, he reaped consolation and singular profit of his labours.

I will set down an example; imitate of it, if you please. For by this means you shall be accustomed to apprehend the presence of God; by this means you shall begin to have your senses sober, watchful, exercised, and calm; by this means you shall prepare yourself a way to the highest contemplation and perfection. Thus, wheresoever you are, you shall spend your time profitably, vague and unstable cogitations being cast forth out of the corners of your heart, and such as are serious being entertained in their place. You may frame yourself meditations and aspirations in other terms than we have. If you perceive the looking in your book to hinder your mind, whereby you are the less able to reach God and to be united to him, lay aside your book. Again, if you perceive it doth farther your exercise, make use of it, for I would that your devotion should be free to you, and that you should follow the grace of the Holy Ghost without confusion or anxiety. Moreover, by aspirations (as you may perceive by the above-written copies) we understand certain short ejaculatory prayers, or burning desires, and lively and loving affections to God. He that hath not as yet undertaken the beginning of internal conversation and his own mortification, or hath at least but newly begun, ought not peradventure so precisely to follow this rule.

But it shall be expedient for him to exercise himself for awhile according to this manner which I shall prescribe. Let him, therefore, every day propose to himself some part of our Saviour's Passion, and let him study to have recourse in mind to the same whether he stand, go, sit, or rest, unless he have some other profitable or necessary thing in his heart to treat of. And let him often discourse with his soul in the presence of Christ suffering, either thus, or after the like manner — O my soul, behold thy God, behold ungrateful, attend thou wretch, consider thou poor soul, behold thy God, behold thy Creator and Redeemer; behold how the King of eternal glory humbled Himself for thee; behold how the highest Majesty debased Himself for thee; see what sorrows, bitterness, and indignities thy Saviour suffereth for thee; consider with what charity He loved thee,

Who undertook so great calamity and affliction for thee. Arise, my soul, arise out of the dust, slip thy head out of the collar, thou captive daughter of Sion. Arise, forsake the puddle of thy vices and leave the uncleanness of thy negligent life. How long wilt thou take pleasure in perils? How long wilt thou esteem anxiety and torments to be rest? How long wilt thou securely sleep in destruction? How long wilt thou willingly leave the right way and wander abroad far and near by unknown places? Return unto the Lord thy God, for He expecteth thee; make haste, be not slack, for He is ready to receive thee; He will meet thee with open arms, only defer not [thou to return. Come to JESUS, and He will heal and purify thee. Join thyself to JESUS, and He will illuminate thee. Adhere to JESUS, and He will bless and save thee. Sometimes let him more expressly upbraid his soul of ingratitude and perverseness, saying—Alas! my soul, how ungrateful hast thou been to thy God. He hath bestowed innumerable and most admirable benefits upon thee, and thou still repayest evil for good. He hath created thee according to His own image and likeness; He hath endowed thee with immortality;

He hath deputed heaven and earth and all things
contained in them to thy commodity; He hath
enriched thee with many gifts and graces; He hath
brought thee to the light of the Catholic faith; He
hath withdrawn thee from the dangerous waves of
the world, and conveyed thee to the haven and
tranquillity of a monastical life, where thou (as in
a most sweet paradise of spiritual pleasures) might
have infinite occasion of holy joy and good works;
He hath patiently borne with thee grievously sinning,
and hath preserved thee from the jaws of hell. The
King hath been incarnate for thee; thy Creator for
thy sake hath become thy Brother. Neither did
He think it sufficient to be born for thee, wherefore
would He also suffer for thy sake. He endured
sorrow and distresses for thy sake; He was betrayed
and taken for thy sake; He was spit on and buffeted
for thy sake; He was scourged and wounded with
a crown of thorns; for thy sake He was smitten
with a reed and laden with the burthen of the
Cross; for thy sake He was nailed to the Cross
and drank vinegar; for thy sake He wept and shed
His most holy blood; for thy sake He died and
was buried. He hath adopted thee to be heir of

the Kingdom of Heaven; He hath promised those things unto thee which neither eye hath seen nor heart of man can comprehend. But thou hast left and condemned Him Who hath been so many ways beneficial to thee; thou hast cast away the holy fear of Him that loved thee; thou hast shaken off His sweet yoke that hath elected thee; thou art become as one of the daughters of Belial, as an impudent harlot; thou hast worshipped iniquities, without modesty; thou hast compacted with death; thou hast given thy hand to the devil; thou hast been most prompt to all wickedness; thou hast heaped evil upon evil, and hast rejoiced to add worse to the worst. By thy wickedness thou hast again crucified JESUS CHRIST, Who hath chosen thee for His spouse; thou hast renewed His wounds by thy crimes. Who will give thee groans and sighs? Who will give thee a spring of tears, that thou mayest night and day bewail thine ingratitude? O unhappy wretch, what wilt thou do? Oh, that thou hadst kept thyself in the state of innocency, and that thou hadst remained immaculate! Oh, that thou hadst not miserably defiled thyself with dishonesty! Oh, that thou hadst not gone astray from thy God! Thou has lost thine innocency; thou art defiled; thou art become dishonest; thou hast gone astray from thy God. Alas! poor wretch, and what wilt thou do? To whom wilt thou fly? From whom wilt thou expect help? From whom but from Him Whom thou hast offended? He is most pitiful, most courteous, most merciful. Humble thyself, pour out thyself like water in His sight, and He will take pity on thee. Sometimes let him turn his lamentations to our Lord with these or the like words—Alas! my Lord JESUS, what have I done! How have I left Thee! How have I despised Thee! How am I become forgetful of Thy name! How have I cast aside Thy name! How have I cast aside Thy fear! How have I trod Thy law under my feet! How have I transgressed Thy precepts. O me, my God! O me, my Creator! O me, my Saviour! O me, my life and my total good! Woe be to me, wretched creature! Woe be to me, woe be to me, because I have sinned! Woe be to me, because I have made myself like to a brute beast! Woe be to me, because I am become more silly than a sheep. O good JESUS, O loving Shepherd, O sweet Master, help me. Set

me on my feet, stretch forth Thy hand to me, being
in danger. Cleanse me from my filth, cure my
wound, confirm my weakness, save me from destruction. I confess myself unworthy to tread on the
earth, I am unworthy to behold the light, I am
unworthy of Thy aid and grace. For great is mine
ingratitude; great, yea, too great, is the enormity
of my sins. Nevertheless, Thy mercy is infinitely
greater. Therefore, O God, Thou lover of mankind,
and my only hope, have mercy on me according to
Thy great mercy, and according to the multitude of
Thy mercies take away mine iniquity. Sometimes,
as if he had risen out of a dream, falling on his
knees in the sight of our Lord, let him affectionately say—Lord, if Thou wilt Thou canst make me
clean. Or this—O God, be propitious to me a
sinner. Or that—Have mercy on me, JESUS, Son of
David. Or that other—O Lord help me. So
likewise let him pour forth his heart before the
Virgin Mary, the Mother of our Lord, and all the
Saints of God, humbly suing for their intercession.

CHAPTER VI.

WE MUST DAILY CALL TO MIND THE MANIFOLD
SINS WHICH WE HAVE COMMITTED.

AND every day, or certainly very often, when
occasion shall serve, let him recollect himself;
and with a profound humility, firmly proposing
amendment, let him call to mind and particularly
confess before our Lord the sins of his forepassed
life, and especially those by which he hath grievously offended the divine goodness. But it will be
indiscreet to dwell long upon those that belong
to the frailty of the flesh, lest the remembrance of
them, and the longer treating of the old sin, breed
a new sin by unlawful delight. In which confession,
contrition, and sensible devotion, let him accustom
himself to lament more that he hath behaved
himself contumeliously and ungratefully towards his
Father and Creator, than that he hath brought
himself in danger of eternal punishment.

In the forms of lamentation and godly complaints which we have prescribed, he need not care for running over many sentences. But let him take what he will, and as many as he will, observing no order; if he make choice of only one, two, or three, whichsoever they be, he may repeat again and again, he shall do well. We would that he should do freely according to his devotion, and always avoiding confusion and perplexity. I know one, that being externally busied in his conversion to our Lord's Passion among chaste discourses took delight to call to mind these few words, or the like: O good JESUS, O pious Pastor, O sweet Master! good JESUS, have mercy on me! pious Pastor, direct me! sweet Master, teach me! my Lord, help me! Another there was that did take delight to run over, sometimes more, sometimes fewer, of the aforesaid lamentations, and express them in diversity of words according to his affection. Let our young beginner, as I have said, be free in these things, and let him stir himself to compunction and diligence in his spiritual purpose by meditating, if he please, upon death, purgatory, judgement, hell, and heaven.

Which kind of meditation, by how much the

nearer it draweth to liberal fear and the love of God, by so much it is the more acceptable to our Lord, and more effectual for the purifying of the soul. Again, by how much the more it participateth of base and servile fear, by so much it is the less profitable. By liberal fear we fear to sin, lest we offend our most bountiful Lord God, and so lose His favour and familiarity. By servile fear we fear to do ill, lest we should undergo damnation and punishment. Nevertheless, it is good to be withdrawn from sinning by servile fear, but so that we stay not there, but pass on to liberal fear. In meditating on eternal. glory, let him go thus, or in the like manner, to work: Oh, how blessed is the heavenly Jerusalem, the walls whereof consist of most precious stones; the gates thereof shine with the most divine pearls; the streets whereof are paved with most pure gold; the gardens similarly being decked with flowers most incomprehensibly flourishing. There the sound of joy is perpetual; there the canticle of gladness is ever sung by an unwearied choir; there the rejoicing of exultation is always renewed; there the instruments of the Saints do always resound; there cinnamon and balm incessantly breathe forth

an unspeakable odour of sweetness; there is peace
and rest overcoming all sense; there is temperate-
ness and calmness beyond all human reach; there
is eternal day and one spirit of all; there is sure
security, secure eternity, eternal tranquillity, quiet
happiness, happy sweetness, and sweet mirth; there
the just shall shine as the sun in the Kingdom
of their Father. Oh, what happiness is it to be
among the choirs of Angels, to have perpetual
fellowship with the holy Patriarchs and Prophets,
with the holy Confessors and Virgins, and with the
most glorious Mother of God! Not to fear, not
to be sorrowful, not to be in anguish, not to be
grieved, not to be troubled with tediousness, to
endure no labour, no impediment, no loathsomeness,
no necessity! Oh, what a wealth of consolation, what
a sea of delights, what an abundance of joys, what
profundity of most pure pleasure will it be to behold
that incircumscriptible light, to see that most amiable
brightness, to see that unspeakable glory of the most
high Trinity, to see the God of Gods in Sion, to
see Him not a riddle, but face to face, to see also
the glorified Humanity of the only-begotten God!
For if the visible bravery of the heavens be a

E

beautiful sight, or to behold the glittering clearness
of the stars, to see the glorious beauty of the sun,
to see the shining of the pale-faced moon, to consider
the grateful light of the air, to contemplate the
elegant neatness of birds, flowers, grass, and colours,
to listen to the sweet chanting of the nightingales
and larks, to hear the melodious harmony of harp
and lute, to smell the fragrant roses and lilies, to
draw the breath that spices and perfume send forth,
to taste the deliciousness of divers palate-pleasing
fruits ; if, I say, there be so great pleasure in these
things, what a torrent of most sincere delight will
it be perfectly to contemplate that immense beauty,
and perfectly to taste that infinite sweetness from
whence all beauty, all sweetness of things created
floweth down to us. The spring-tide representeth
unto us the state of eternal felicity, ˙ and the
future resurrection ; for when we see heaven, earth,
trees, and all things else with a certain new grace
to be decked with admirable ornaments ; notwithstanding, there is greater difference between that
which it representeth than between noon and mid-
night. Blessed, therefore, yea, thrice blessed, is that
heavenly Jerusalem where nothing wanteth that may

please, and whence all things are banished that may displease, where Almighty God is happily praised for ever. Let him learn purely to frequent the joys of this supernal city, to love and desire them, yet not so much for his own profit, as for the profit and honour of God. Although, indeed, the meditation of eternal life may be more sincerely practical by him that hath been a proficient in internal conversation, than by him that hath scarcely attained to the beginning of his own mortification, and knoweth better how to seek himself than God. In our above-related meditation let a novice exercise himself continually for the space of one, three, or six months, yea, for a whole year or more; until he perceive within himself an absolute contempt of the world and himself, and that he beginneth to feel the fervent purpose of a spiritual life to take root in him. Some are with more difficulty, some more easily turned to the better. And some, whom it pleaseth God out of His most infinite favour most liberally to prevent, are presently changed. In the meantime he may also employ himself in thanksgiving, in praising God, and other prayers; but let his chief employment be in reasonable mourning for, and persecuting

E 2

of, his sins. Let him not be troubled if he cannot draw tears externally, for he lacketh not tears internally that truly hateth all sin and iniquity.

Now after he hath in some measure reformed the image of God within himself by healthful bitterness of mourning and contrition, he may with greater confidence and profit imitate the above proposed example of exercise.

Therefore let him take courage, and fervently prepare himself for a more intimate familiarity with the heavenly Bridegroom. But as long as he is weak or cold he shall kindle in himself the fire of divine love by serious meditation on the Incarnation or Passion of the only-begotten Son of God, sweetly conferring with his soul concerning these things. By which meditation being once inflamed, let him compose himself by prayer and aspiration, desiring by them to unite his spirit to the chiefest good. If he often persist by this means to draw his heart to the love of God, he shall soon bring himself to that pass that presently, at the first convention of his mind or aspiration, without any premeditation he may be able to separate himself from creatures and their imagination, and plunge himself in the sweetness of divine love.   Then he shall not so much need to remember each particular sin of his life past in his penance before God, and with sorrow to direct the insight of his heart unto Him, for so might his freedom and affection towards good be hindered; but rather let him lovingly direct his heart to God Himself, detesting whatsoever may separate or withdraw him from Him.   Neither do we mean that he should negligently forget his sins, but so to remember them that the remembrance hinder not a greater profit; therefore let him confess them daily to God, rather summarily than particularly.

Truly we have a more present remedy against lesser sins when we turn to God by a sweet and effectual affection of love, than when we tediously busy ourselves in the consideration of them and severe punishment of them.   Let him therefore cast them away into the bottomless depth of God's divine mercy and goodness, that, like a sparkle of fire in the midst of the sea, they may there perish. Let him endeavour to reject quite and clean all inordinate pusillanimity, and superfluous scruples of conscience, and perplexed diffidence, whensoever

they arise. For unless they be presently lopped off
they do divers ways choke up the alacrity of the
mind, and very much hinder our internal going
forward.

CHAPTER VII.

EVERY ONE OUGHT TO CONSIDER HIS OWN ABILITY, AND TO PROCEED ACCORDINGLY.

MOREOVER, let him attempt nothing beyond his strength, but be content with his lot. If he cannot reach as far as he desireth, let him reach as far as he can. And unless he flatter himself, he may easily know what proceedings he is able to make. Nevertheless, the divine bounty is liberal, infusing itself wheresoever it findeth a mind worthily prepared.

Wherefore, if our spiritual practitioner be not yet admitted to the sublimity of contemplation and perfect charity, let him think himself as yet not prepared for the receipt of so great a good. And what good would it do him to receive that grace, which he knows not how to make good use of. Let him make haste to pull up all vice by the root, that he may be the fitter. But still with this proviso, that he strive not beyond his strength. Let him not impatiently try to forerun God's grace,

but humbly to follow it.   Let him not, I say,
violently force his spirit thither, whither he cannot
reach ; lest presuming, which he ought not, he tumble
himself down headlong by his own violence, and
being crushed be punished for his rashness.   Let him
so tend to perfection, that unbridled violence and
turbulent solicitude bear no part in his endeavours.

Let him attend the measure of grace given him,
and withal remember that he shall far more easily,
safely, quickly, and happily attain to the highest
degree of contemplation, that is, to the comprehend-
ing of mystical divinity, if he be touched and rapt
by the mere grace of God, than if he endeavour to
attain unto it by his own labours.   Let him always,
therefore, observe a man with discretion, lest by
excess he run into defects.

The bread of tears is good, and many, when
they should refresh themselves, surfeit by it.   For
they insist so long in tears, and with so great
confusion and agitation, that both spirit and body
are fain to lie down under the too much intent or
extended exercise.   We confess that many, by the
discretion and the help of the Holy Ghost, can long
and profitably mourn ; and there are many again

that being, as it were, steeped in the torrent of pleasure which they take in God, do unseasonably urge and spur forward themselves to greater violence, and desist not from this indiscreet forcing of themselves until, being hurt and confounded, they fall and faint in themselves, and are thenceforth made unapt to receive the sweetness of grace. Wherefore the internal heat and violence is always so to be moderated, that the spirit be not extinguished, but comforted by it. They whose heads are of a good temper may more fervently and strongly insist in fervent aspirations; but they that have weak heads (especially if the weakness grow by indiscretion) are not able to exercise themselves otherwise than very gently and moderately. And such can scarcely sometimes admit a simple compunction of mind, or meditation, or reading, without hurt, yea, although they leave their head on some place. So great is the calamity of the vice that proceedeth from indiscretion. But let them diligently, inasmuch as in them lieth, avoid this discommodity, and humbly pray to God for the restoring of that which they have spoiled themselves. If God be pleased to hear them, let them be thankful; if not, let them bless

our Lord, and for His love learn according to His
pleasure patiently to endure this misery, which they
have done on themselves.

Let our internal practitioner beware also of all
lightness of inconstancy and instability. Let him
take in hand those exercises that are good; and
let him go on with what he hath once begun,
although they like him not; but so that the pleasure
of the Holy Ghost be followed in all, the decree
of his own will and appointment being rejected.
For the Holy Ghost doth divers ways as it were
invite us and uses to bring us by divers paths to the
wine-cellar and bed-chamber of divine love; Whose
instinct we must still observe and most readily
follow, laying aside all propriety; wherefore this
our spiritual scholar shall often present himself to
the Holy Ghost as a prepared instrument; and
which way soever the Holy Ghost shall bend and
apply, let him presently follow. If at any time
he shall be drawn or elevated up to the soaring
contemplation and embracements of the chiefest
good, let him freely offer up himself; and if
the Passion of Christ, or any holy meditation and
imagination occur, let him not stay at it, but with

all expedition fly thither, whither he is called by the Spirit.

When he doubtfully staggereth in his purpose, not knowing how he ought to proceed in his begun enterprize, let him use the counsel of men that are prudent, expert, and humble; for so he shall be a greater proficient, than if relying upon himself he proceed according to his own inventions.

But in the meantime let him not forget carefully to have recourse to the remedy of prayer, humbly beseeching in all things to be directed and illuminated by our Lord; lest at any time being deceived he follow error instead of truth. And let him always remember that he can never perfectly be at leisure for God, unless his heart be free and clear from all things besides God.

You have now heard, Brother, after a manner, how he should begin and how he should go forward in external exercises that desireth to attain to any excellent degree of a pure life. It shall be your part not only to hear and read these things, but also to put them in practice. Which if you do, and have help from above, and that you being to be clear within, and that psalmodies and other offices of divine praise wax sweet unto you, search not too high, but be afraid. For although, your heart being enlarged, you do awhile run the way of God's commandments, you have not of yourself enlarged your heart, but God hath done it. And He that enlarged it can permit it, His grace being withdrawn, to be again coupled up and imprisoned. The Sun of Justice hath shined on you, and certain scales being taken off, hath illuminated your mind; but who can hinder Him from hiding Himself if He be so pleased. Be you therefore ready; for He will hide Himself, and His amiable brightness being once departed, your senses shall again be darkened and hindered.

Moreover, certain immissions by evil angels will toss the ship of your breast; yea, peradventure the temptation will be so strong, that you will think all to oppose itself against you. You will seem to yourself to be wholly given over to Satan, and will not have list to open your mouth in God's praise. Neither shall this calamity endure a little while. Neither shall you only once, or thrice, or six, or ten times be laid hold on by it, but very often, sometimes more vehemently than at others. But be not dejected at this ; neither think anything sinisterly of your fault. For He hath permitted you to be tempted that it may be manifest if you truly love Him, and that you may learn to pity others that are oppressed by temptations. He scourgeth and bruiseth you, that He may purge you from vice, and prepare you for more grace. He seemeth to leave you, as it were, for a time, that you wax not proud, but may always acknowledge that you can do nothing without Him ; yet, nevertheless, He doth not forsake you. He exerciseth you in these and the like adversities out of the unspeakable charity wherewith He loveth you. For the Heavenly Spouse useth this kind of dispensation with a fervent soul converted unto Him. He visiteth her solemnly in the beginning of her new purpose, doth comfort and illustrate her, and after He hath recreated and allured her with His sweet smile, he draweth her after Him, and lovingly meeteth her almost everywhere, with His milk feeding His new friend.

Afterwards He begins to administer to her the solid food of affliction, and plainly shows her how much she ought to endure for His name. Now she beginneth to be in a sea of troubles. Men molest

her without, passions trouble her within. Punishments afflict her externally, internally she becometh
dejected by pusillanimity. Externally she is grieved
with infirmities, internally darkness overcasteth and
cloudeth her. The external parts are oppressed, the
internal dried up ; one while the Bridegroom hideth
Himself from the soul, another while He discovereth
Himself unto her. Now He leaveth her, as it were,
in the darkness and horror of death, and presently
recalleth her to the sweetness of light, insomuch that
it may be truly said of Him that He leadeth down to
hell and bringeth back again. By such means He
trieth, purifieth, humbleth, teacheth, weans, draws,
and adorns the soul If He find her faithful in all
things, and to be of a good will and holy patience,
and that, by long exercise and His grace, she doth
mildly and affectionately endure all tribulations and
temptations, then doth He more perfectly join her to
Himself, and similarly maketh her partaker of His
secrets, and bindeth her far otherwise to Him. This
He did at the beginning of her conversion. Be
not therefore troubled when vehement temptation
scourgeth you, but as if you received a token of His
love remain faithful and invincible in your agonies,

saying with blessed Job—'"Although He shall kill me I will trust in Him" during this storm. It will be somewhat hard for you to be present at the Divine Office, by reason of the instability and cloudiness of your mind. Notwithstanding, be patient, and gently do what lieth in your power. The night will pass away, darkness will be dispersed, and light will take place again. But as long as it is yet night take heed you are not found idle and negligent; if you have no list to pray, sing, or meditate, then read. If your mind loathe reading, write, or manfully exercise yourself for the time in some other external work, in the meantime diligently rejecting the troubles of vain cogitations. If drowsiness do unseasonably molest you, so that it grievously depress you, you shall peradventure (time and place permitting) do better if somewhat pertinently, to the honour of God, leaning your head somewhere, you slumber a little, than if inexorably you resist it; for if by labour you think to drive it away, as long as you labour you shall be free, but that once past, and you betaking yourself to your spiritual exercises, it will easily return. If you sleep, let it not be deep nor long, so that it last no longer than one may say one, or two, or three Psalms : for so your spirit, being, as it were, renewed, will arise with more expedition and alacrity. They that know not how to behave themselves soberly in eating, drinking, and the custody of their senses, if they fly to this remedy it is to be feared lest they rather aggravate than alleviate this disease, and, falling into a deep and long sleep, miserably lose their time by sluggishness. Watch carefully against those temptations by which the devil endeavoureth to incline the mind to those things that are indecent and vicious. Be sure to reject them in the very beginning, before they take possession of you within, for unless you repel the adversary at the first onset, if he get entrance he will presently clap bolts on your soul, and you, being destitute of liberty and force, will hardly be able to resist. But if you have behaved yourself negligently, and he fetter you, do not yield so, but deny your consent, and strive against him even by creeping on the ground, and pray to our Lord in the strength of your spirit, that, freeing your bonds, he will restore you to liberty, or at least preserve you from giving consent. But know that many times you shall more easily overcome the adversary suggesting any filthy, impious, and absurd thing, if you contemn and set light by his barking, and so pass them over, than if you strive long with him, and with great labour endeavour to stop his wicked mouth. But if he over much importune you, and being repelled once or twice do still come on afresh, you must meet with him on plain terms, that, being overthrown on plain ground, he may fly away with disgrace.

Now, he setteth on us many ways, for sometimes he seeketh to ensnare us secretly, and under pretence of piety; sometimes he setteth upon us openly and with open fury; sometimes he creepeth by little; sometimes he breaketh forth suddenly and unlooked for; sometimes he layeth siege to us by spiritual and internal means, sometimes by corporal and external adversaries or prosperities. Wherefore we must always have recourse to the aid of our Lord's Passion, and cry to God with tears. But, as I have always said, soar not too high by reason of the grace which, peradventure, you have. For what have you that you have not received? Why do you glory, as if you had not received? Take heed, therefore, that by no means you open the window

F

of your heart to the blast of vainglory or the air of self-complacence. See you brag not, see you boast not abroad of what you have received. But keep your secret to yourself, let it abide with you, unless you happen to reveal it humbly and modestly to some intimate and secret friend for spiritual utility and consolation, or that you be compelled by obedience, or rather manifest necessity, or great profit. See that you believe not that you have received the gift of God by your own merits and labours, but rather judge yourself unworthy (as indeed you are) of all grace and consolation, and worthy of all confusion and dereliction. Compare yourself with those that are more holy, that, by consideration of their perfection, you may the better acknowledge your own imperfection. Humble and deject yourself; place yourself infinitely below all men. But you will say, How can I do this, considering that many without fear or shame live most debauchedly, which I neither do nor will do? What! shall I cast myself below them? Shall I place them above me? I say you shall.

CHAPTER VIII.

A VERY GOOD MEANS TO OBTAIN HUMILITY.

FOR if you consider that these who to-day are so bad may to-morrow be more perfect than yourself, and that, if they had received the gifts that are granted you from above they would lead a far more holy life than yourself, and that you would sin more grievously than they if you were not prevented by a more abundant grace; I say, if you consider these things you will easily observe how fit it. were that you should prefer every sinner before yourself. Oh, if you did know the secret of God, how willingly would you give place to others; how gladly would you take the lowest place; how joyfully would you lay yourself at the feet of others; with what alacrity would you attend the sick; how devoutly would you honour all; how affectionately obedient would you be, without any delay or complaint. But yet I require a more

F 2

excellent thing of you, viz., that you place yourself
not only below all men in your heart for God's
sake, but also below each creature, reputing yourself
as most abject dust, esteeming yourself unworthy to
tread on the earth or to enjoy the benefit of light.
Look more exactly into yourself—how ungrateful,
tepid, unstable, miserable, and vile you are, and by
that means you will attain to that most humble
submission of mind.   If the old enemy knock
importunately at the door of your heart, putting
into your conceit that you should think yourself
somebody, that you should vainly glory and compare
yourself with others, repel the subtle villany, lock
the doors against him, and although you feel some
pestilent immissions, beware always of giving your
consent; for if you consent, if you let in the
impostor, and incline your mind to his unlawful
allurements, you have broken your faith and vow,
which you have made to the Bridegroom of your
soul; you have polluted the bed of your Beloved,
which before flourished; neither can you be admitted
to His most blessed familiarity unless you cast out
the adulterer and humble yourself exceedingly.   And,
peradventure, you shall not be received to favour

unless you be first punished and afflicted for awhile, and that the filthy kisses which the impure spirit hath imprinted on your soul be razed out by the scourge of God. But enough hath been spoken of this.

CHAPTER IX.

HITHERTO we have spoken how you ought to assist at the Divine Office, what internal exercises you should undertake, what rule to be observed, what to be followed, what to be avoided in them. We will now pass to the rest that we have to speak of. As for corporal refections, beware of all excess, lest, being overladen, you be made inapt for all spiritual exercises. For it cannot be but that the belly, swelling by intemperance, must needs draw away the mind from God and those things that belong to salvation. Wine especially, being more largely used, although without drunkenness, is a great impediment. It inflameth the body, confoundeth the internal parts, and, distressing the alacrity of the spirit, stirreth up a beastly kind of sluggishness. In vain, therefore, doth that man aspire to a spiritual life that yieldeth to his belly ; lop off, therefore, all vicious desires. Take no care whether your meat or drink be very delicate or sweet of itself. It it be man's meat, and reasonable, what need you desire more? You are a Monk: come then to the table to refresh your body of God's gifts, not to nourish the pleasures of the flesh. Wherefore, if you are troubled about the goodness of your victuals, and do murmur, as I have already said, so I say again—you are no Monk. If JESUS were truly pleasing to your heart, what poor fare for His sake would not be pleasing to your palate. For JESUS is a more pleasant sauce, even to extreme poverty. Love Him, and all manner of food will not be less, nay, will be more, pleasing unto you than the delicious banquets of Kings. JESUS, being hungry for your sake, was often fed with bare bread ; JESUS, thirsting for your sake, drank vinegar and gall. Take your meat and drink continently, leisurely, and moderately, excluding all brutish greediness. Have a care even of the natural delight that proceedeth from your natural refection. Do not reflect upon it, do not desire to feed your sensuality, for if you feed that it will feed on you and pollute you within. And as you must often deny the flesh what it evilly desireth, so sometimes you must force it to receive what it desireth not. For sometimes it doth in a manner loathe that which natural necessity requireth.

Furthermore, beware that, while you refresh your body, your mind be not in the meantime hunger-starved. Therefore let the mouth of your heart feed on the word of God, and let your ears receive the wholesome doctrine and deeds of the Saints. And if you happen to sit at that table where there is no holy reading, do not thus deprive yourself of your spiritual food, but, as much as silence will permit, converse inwardly either with your soul or with God, and propose to yourself some godly thing to keep yourself doing. As in your diet, so be also in your apparel. Reject, scorn, and detest whatsoever is contrary to monastical simplicity. Neither do you imitate those vain and wretched Monks that are ashamed of their estate and vocation, but not of their lewd life and conversation; who, if they are to go abroad and to come into the sight of seculars, will bewray their foolishness and curiosity. They must, forsooth, have such and such clothes, and wear their cassock after this or that fashion. They are ashamed to wear their apparel according as religion doth ordain, and according to the Constitutions of their Superiors and ancestors. And coming abroad, not like humble Monks, but like delicate and neat courtiers, by this prodigious sight they provoke wise men to sorrow and indignation, but find matter of mirth for the devil, evidently showing by this absurdity what they are within, viz., proud, wanton, and full of vainglory. Alas! wretched Monks, far wide from the scope of true religion. O Monks — not Monks, but monsters! O Monks detestable, by being thus deluded by the devil's clothing. Is this it that you promised to God, when, by the most sacred vow of poverty, you solemnly renounced the world, with all the pomps and vanities thereof? Is this it that the King of Kings hath taught you by His word? Is this it that He hath showed by His example, when, being wrapped in base clouts, He had no other cradle than a manger; when, likewise, He was apparelled in a white garment and a purple robe in scorn? Is this to follow JESUS? Is this to follow JESUS' footsteps? O intolerable confusion! O extremity of madness! Look to yourself, Brother, that you become not like these, but rather be content with plain apparel, whether you be within the monastery or without, for thus much your profession exacteth of you. Everywhere, but especially during the Divine Office, keep your eyes from wandering, neither lightly look about you either this way or that, unless necessity require, lest you chance to see something that may hinder you from attention and purity of heart. But although there be no fear of danger, yet monastical discipline requireth that, whether you rest or go, you use modestly to look down upon the ground. Never look curiously on the face of any.

Let not your gait be too swift or hasty, especially in the Church, unless it happen of necessity that it must be so. Neither out of the Church let it be overdone, or remiss, but modest and civil. In all things compose yourself to a laudable carriage of your whole body.

Let your looks before others be pleasing, with a decent gravity, behaving yourself courteously and affably towards all. And if against your will you happen to be over-sorrowful, so dissemble it that you seem not unpleasant and harsh, and so be troublesome to the rest. When you are forced to laugh, laugh sparingly and like a Monk. Avoid long laughter as a great impediment to you in your purpose, and as the destruction of your soul ; knowing that vehement and immoderate laughter doth violate the cloisters of modesty, and, dispersing the interior powers of the soul, driveth the grace of the Holy Ghost out of your heart.

Above all things, love solitude, silence, and taciturnity. Be more ready to hear than to speak. Be not hasty, nor turbulent, nor clamorous, nor contentious in words ; but speak modestly, bashfully, courteously, and, without dissembling, what is true and right. Be not, I say, too loud ; nor yet so low that you cannot be understood, especially if the place, time, cause, or person to whom you speak require that you speak somewhat more loud than ordinary ; for, as the voice of a Monk should always be bashful, and for the most part low, according to the holy ordinations of religion, so also sometimes it ought to be reasonably loud. Affirm nothing obstinately, unless matter of faith or necessity of salvation constrain ; but whosoever contradicteth you, either yield or hold your peace ; if neither ought to be done, affirm with modesty and humility what you know to be certain ; for by this means you shall take away all occasion of.

irreligious contention.   Let not your words be biting.
Willingly speak not anything that may be either to
your own credit or others discommendation.   But if,
out of necessity or utility, you speak any such thing,
do it with a laudable modesty and a pure intention.
Abhor dissolute tales as the poison of the soul   As
for jests (if they happen in your presence), albeit you
suffer them, yet relate them not.   Never consent to a
tongue that speaketh foolishly, unseemly, and perniciously.   Yea, if such things are spoken, do you, if
it seem good, mildly and with reason find fault with
the speaker; if you think it not good, yet at least
cut off his speech honestly and endeavour to draw
him to better discourse: if, possibly, you may
give no ear to backbiters.   The liberty of external
recreation granted you, either by walking or other
wise, see you abuse not; that is, make such use of
them that they hinder not your spiritual going
forward, but rather further it   You may, indeed, to
the honour of God slake your mind, but let it not
loose, lest, whilst you wander abroad, being expelled
out of yourself, some delight or passion contrary to
the spirit lay hold on you, and disperse your interior
senses and replenish them with bitterness.   Therefore

carefully learn, by a certain advised simplicity of mind, to abide within yourself, that the noise of vain cogitations and the motion of inordinate affections being represented, you may keep your heart in silence and liberty. Let God be your chief, yea, your whole thought and study, for it is not enough for you that He be your whole intention.

Likewise, in all external occupations endeavour that, with Martha, you do not only for the honour of God perform your work prudently, devoutly, and with alacrity, but that also in those works which you faithfully do to the honour of God, with Mary, you direct your mind, being freed from the tumult of cogitations and the confused imagination of sensible things, to God, or those things that are divine, especially if reasonable discourse or any other necessity hinder not.

CHAPTER X.

MARTHA, because she is distracted in her external actions and in her right intentions by the multiplicity of vain cogitations, and is troubled about many things, although peradventure she be not deformed, yet is she not comely enough. But Mary, because she knoweth how to forsake the troops of unstable cogitations, and persisting in unity and tranquillity of mind, doth strive to cleave to goodness itself, is of more perfect beauty. Wherefore howsoever you are externally occupied, love not only to be right and innocent with Martha, but also to be clear and simple with Mary. Mary hath chosen the better part, which shall not be taken away from her. And you have chosen the same; which unless you keep, according to your power, you produce not fruit worthy your profession. Have therefore always a charitable simplicity of mind if you be yet a little one in Christ, and are not able to follow Mary, soaring so high in mind; imitate her humility, imitate her affectionate watering our Lord's feet with tears, imitate her most lovingly seeking our Lord in the sepulchre. For even in these she had simplicity of mind; she loved one thing, she thought on pne thing, she sought one thing. But imitate her not for your own delight, but to please our Lord. For if by spiritual delectation you do principally seek yourself in these, your soul is not the chaste spouse of Christ, but the most base servant of sin; I might say, the devil's impure hackney. You shall at length merit to be admitted to the apprehension of higher mysteries by these that are more low, if I may so call them, which, indeed, are not low, but of a wondrous height.

In all things that differ not from the sincerity of a monastical life, conform yourself to the Community, still avoiding vicious irregularity. And because you live among Monks that live laudably according to the sweet austerity of a holy Rule, be not singular in abstinence and watching; neither exceed the rest of the Monks therein, unless by the revelation of the Holy Ghost you know it to be the will and pleasure of God. Neither attempt anything without the counsel and consent of your Superior, lest, while you presume of your own head to afflict your body beyond measure, you make yourself unable for good works, and wholly deprive yourself of the fruit of your labour. God requireth of you purity of mind, not the overthrow of your body. He would that you should subject it to the spirit, not oppress it. Therefore, as well in external exercises as internal, temper the fervour of your mind with a holy discretion.

If your will, being more slow to virtue and remiss, do, as it were, sleep, rouse it up, spur it forward. But if, having too much bridle, it run too fast, repress and check it. Always assist it with holy fear in the presence of God. And let these words always resound in the ears of your heart—"Look to thyself." Consider not over-curiously the deeds of others, what are their manners and behaviour, unless it belong unto you as an officer. Let your curiosity and business be about yourself. Howbeit, think not in this that I would have you make no account of the excesses or sins of others, or neglect to amend them as much as in you lieth, or procure them to be amended. For we condemn curiosity, not holy zeal of justice. We discommend not what in this case is not against mature stability, or contrary to the sincere love of your neighbour. These vices that you see in others, or hear of them, either think them not to be simply true, or interpret them in the better part; but if they be so manifest that no interpretation can qualify them, endeavour to separate your sight both of body and mind from them, and reflecting on your own sins, if you have leisure, humbly pray to God both for yourself and them. For so shall you more easily avoid unquiet suspicions and rash judgements. But beware that with consent of reason you rejoice not at another's sin, though of small moment, or of any adversity; but mourn for your brother before our Lord, calling to mind that we are members one of another, all one body, and redeemed all with the same blood. Learn not to be angry, but to pity the defects of others, and patiently to bear with them, whether they be defects of body or mind.

For it is written, "Bear one another's burdens;" and so you shall fulfil the law of Christ. Let not

G

the heavenly grace which you observe in others excite
you to satanical envy, but to a faithful imitation and
godly congratulation.   And although you have not
the, spiritual good that you know another to be
blessed with, yet rejoice in heart that God is honoured
by it: as readily thank our Lord for it as if it were
your own.

And, indeed, it will be to your own good, and you
shall be crowned for another's as for your own.   Nay,
more; it shall become your own.   So order your
mind that you desire not to please the world, nor fear
to displease it.   In man, although very nearly allied,
love nothing but good, or the grace and workmanship
of good.   And again, hate nothing but vice.

Offend not God willingly, either for kinsmen,
friends, or any other body's sake, though never so
well deserving at your own hands; neither favour,
flatter, or applaud any one in any sin.   Do not
earnestly desire the presence or speech of any man
unless it be for some spiritual good; and yet a
perplexed earnestness is neither, then, good.   Love
all men, but spiritually, not sensually.   For so it
will come to pass, that you will not be inordinately
troubled at the corporal absence of such as are

virtuous or your friends, nor afflicted at the corporal presence of such as are vicious or your enemies.

Nay, esteem no man your enemy, but love even your persecutors, as the most dear furtherers of your salvation. Whatsoever you see, hear, or perceive in creatures to be delightful and worthy of singular admiration, either by their natural disposition, or the art and industry of man, refer it to the praise of the great Creator, or the use of eternal beatitude, that you may be delighted in our Lord. Always be afraid of sensual delectation, whencesoever it hath its beginning. For if you seek yourself by that and cleave to it, you will be entangled and defiled. Utterly detest the love of all sinners, yea, even of the very least. By which, notwithstanding, if, peradventure, being overreached, you fall out of frailty, afflict not yourself unreasonably with inordinate pusillanimity, but humbly confess your fault before our Lord, and renewing your good purpose and piously taking heart, cast all your defects into the unsearchable profundity of His mercies or His most holy wounds. As long as you live in this clay building of your body, you may mortify in yourself the affections of lesser sinners, but wholly avoid to slip into them you cannot. Godly Monks, although they slip sometimes, yea, very often, yet they hate sinning and beware of it, and grieve after they have offended; but perverse Monks sin without hating, without bewailing of it. For they take no pains to extinguish the affections of lesser faults, nor to avoid the occasion of them. They desire the liberty of a more loose life; they love to be absent from Divine Office and other conventual acts; they desire delicate and superfluous meat and drink; they espy out opportunities of trifling; they affect inordinate laughter. They delight in secular businesses, to see vanities, to have curious things for their own use: self-complacence, foolish joy, idleness, vain talk, fables, fantastic behaviour, and such other vices are with them not at all, or scarcely accounted, faults; in their conscience they make no bones of them. For being made insensible, they think themselves whole when they are deeply wounded, and, therefore, neither care for lamenting their sins, nor amending their life. But what say they? These, say they, are no wounds, or if they be, they are very little ones, and as much as nothing. O wretched Monks! O mad Monks! O Monks, not Monks! For although they seem little, yet, because they are not afraid to receive them, and after receipt of them defer to cure them, they become mortal. I speak nothing of their falling into pride, rebellion, disobedience, murmurings, fury, detractions, hatred, envy, contempt, gluttony, with other hideous sins, and all by this negligence. Do not, Brother, do not imitate these; for they are not disciples of the Crucified, and the beloved friends of God; neither. ever shall be, unless they leave off to be what they are. Look you better to yourself, leave, remove, cast aside whatsoever may any way hinder you from the true love of God.

CHAPTER XI.

BY mortification, as by a certain and compendious
way, hasten to perfection of life. Will you in few
words know what this generality of mortification is?
Will you know that only certain short cut? I will
tell you; I will show you. Give ear therefore. Put
off all propriety. Behold this short way. Put off
all propriety. And what is the meaning of this?
Lay aside all you own will and seeking; put off
all the old man. ' But that you may the better
understand what is spoken, I will propose the same
a little more plainly.

Have you bound yourself to the observance of
poverty? Why, then, be poor. Poor, how is that?
Be poor in the desire of wealth and passions of
the mind, poor in spirit. If you love and desire
anything by propriety of affection and sensuality;

if as yet you seek yourself in anything, you are yet voluntary, you are not yet truly poor ; you cannot yet, with St. Peter, say to God, "So we have left all, and have followed Thee." Strip yourself, leave all, put off all propriety. Whatsoever is not God, let not abide in your heart by cleaving to it, or inordinately loving it. Be free from all things that are besides God ; insomuch, that I would have you neither foolishly to rejoice for any good news, nor to be inordinately dejected for any bad ; and whether you have not received what you yet have not, or have lost what you have, every way keep a stable and quiet state of mind. For God's sake utterly deny all sensible things, yea, even yourself. Which is as much as to say, mortify in yourself the force of concupiscence, delight, anger, and natural indignation ; and as well in adversity as prosperity resign yourself over to God's divine pleasure, without any contradiction of will. I have showed you that this short way and general mortification of yourself in none other than the general casting away of all propriety, that is, a humiliation of yourself in all kinds. For, indeed, perfect humility itself is that shortest way, by which

you go straightforward to the port of perfection.
Now this port is perfect charity, or purity. You
will demand how you may know whether you have
attained to that port. I will give you manifest
instructions. If always abiding in silence of heart,
as in a most quiet haven, you affectionately direct
and incline towards God your mind, being free from
all inordinate care, affection, and earnest imagination
of things that are below you, and, in a word, from
all disquiet and tumult, so that your memory, your
understanding, your will—that is, your whole spirit—
possessing the above-named port, be happily united
to God.

This is the sum of all perfection. For although,
being clothed with this corruptible flesh, we cannot
always by present insight and memory stick to the
theory and speculation of God, yet here we ought
always to be fixed by our intention; and hither,
as to a mark, we ought carefully to recall our mind
as often as we waste ourselves by unseasonable,
light, and unsettled cogitations. As long as by
reading, meditating, hearing, or speaking, we profitably and sincerely treat of any contemplative and
spiritual matter, we are not separated from God.

Neither when, occasion requiring, we do with the like sobriety and sincerity speak or think of external matters in their due time, do we go far from God. Oh, what a brave philosopher, what a wise man, what an excellent divine shall I account you; oh, how happy and blessed, if you convey these things by your corporal ears into the ears of your heart, and, being stirred up to the true mortification of yourself, do lay the axe to the root of the tree. But what tree is this? It is propriety, of which we spake a little before. But what is the axe, then? It is the fervour of spiritual and internal exercise. But chiefly the daily handling of our Lord's Passion, and often aspirations to God, with prompt obedience and a reasonable sobriety of diet, are this axe. It is certainly a sharp axe, a blessed axe, a most grateful axe, an axe that bringeth with it all good and all purity, a golden axe, and decked with precious stones. But the tree is a cursed tree, a tree full of most bitter fruits, a tree of all evil, a tree that produceth and nourisheth all inordinateness, a tree of obscurity and darkness. This tree is in you, as also in all others, and as long as it abideth in you, your cannot have perfect light. If,

therefore, you desire clearly to behold the bright
beams of the Sun of Justice, cut down this tree and
cast it from you. It is a very thick and hard tree,
not to be cut down at the first blow, nor the first day,
nor, perchance, the first year; no, nor peradventure
in a long time together. Wherefore, perseverance
and patience are requisite. Now, as gold, if there be
no let, naturally goeth downwards, and the flame of
fire is carried upwards, so the mind that is purged
and purified from the dross of propriety, and seeketh
only the will of God, is naturally elevated to her
beginning, which is God, and is more freely united
to Him; but the mind that is partly purged of it,
although she tend to her beginning, and be in some
sort illustrated from above by the brightness of
eternal light, yet, notwithstanding, because all impediment is not taken away, she cannot have free
passage nor flow to, nor be swallowed up in, the
bottomless depth of eternal light; that is, she cannot
freely be united to God, her principal and greatest
good. Furthermore, although God out of His bounty
be pleased sometimes to lift up some to His love by
a more easy way without many temptations, yet let
no man, although enriched with spiritual gifts, easily

believe that he hath attained to the perfect resigna-
tion of himself, unless in very deed he has endured
many most grievous adversities, and has kept a
perfect quietness and liberty of mind in the toleration
of them. There are many that, as long as they feel
no checks, no injuries, no losses, no temptations, no
troubles, seem devout, patient, and humble; but, as
soon as they are once touched by them, they proudly
show, by murmuring, indignation, and impatience,
how little they are mortified. Wherefore, before any
one can be thought to have attained to the true
abnegation of himself, he must necessarily endure
many adversities with a voluntary and quiet mind.
And as for him that hath been exactly tried by God
in afflictions, let him think that he hath not yet gone
so far as that he is able to endure them; for if he
had, without doubt he should not want occasions of
diverse tribulations; for God rejoiceth to adorn the
soul more secretly and perfectly joined to Him with
manifold afflictions, as it were with so many precious
pearls, and so to bring it to the true similitude of
JESUS CHRIST. He, therefore, that, rejecting propriety in all things, conformeth his will to the divine
will and ordinance, being equally prepared to undergo

any adversity, confusion, subtraction of internal sweetness for God's sake, as he would the affluence of any
prosperity, honour, and devotion; he, I say, that is
come to that pass, that he can endure all temptation
and tribulation with a certain internal sweetness and
joy, this man hath found a precious pearl; this man
hath attained to the highest degree of perfection; he
is everywhere, and in all occasions, united to God,
and most sweetly poureth his soul to Him. He doth
purely, quietly, simply, joyfully, and sweetly walk all
the day long in the light of our Lord's countenance,
and can adhere to highest contemplation when he
pleaseth with the same facility that he doth live and
breathe. What in this vale of misery he may receive
from Heaven, and to what God will be pleased fami-
liarly to admit him, it lieth not in our power to speak,
for, indeed, they are things unspeakable. Let him
that is such glorify God, and confess that JESUS
CHRIST hath raised up the needy from the earth,
and lifted up the poor out of the dung, since that
of an impure man here on earth He hath made an
Angel like to God.

CHAPTER XII.

A MONK OR NUN, BY VIRTUE OF THEIR PROFESSION,
IS BOUND TO TEND TO PERFECTION.

YOU will, peradventure, say, Oh, this perfection is too much above me, therefore will I not stretch myself, nor endeavour to apprehend it, lest I should labour in vain. But my answer is, that if you do according to your words, you are no Monk; for, although you are not bound to attain to perfection, yet are you bound, as much as in you lieth, to endeavour to attain to it. Flatter yourself how you will, persuade yourself as you will, fain and pretend what excuses you will, you are bound with might and main to tend to perfection. It is even so and not otherwise. If hitherto you have been ignorant of it, henceforth ignorance cannot excuse you; you have bound and obliged yourself, and so you shall remain.

But you will say, I cannot attain to such perfection. What mean you by this distrust? Are you ignorant that the divine power can do more than human infirmity can imagine? I confess that of yourself you cannot attain it, but God is able to bring you. Believe God, hope in God, not in yourself. Trust in the grace and help of God, not in your own endeavours. Nevertheless, that God may be with you, be not you wanting to yourself by sloth. Do what lieth in your power, put forth your hands, stretch out your arms, confirm your mind to the destruction of vice, to the perfect abnegation of yourself; recollect your heart, produce affection, elevate your mind to the contemplation of those things that are eternal, and accustom yourself everywhere to attend the presence of God : which that you may the better perform, propose to yourself according to the above demonstrated example every day some part of our Lord's Passion, and carefully cast your internal eyesight upon the same ; in the meantime sweetly conversing with JESUS, or with your soul concerning Him. Always, I say, busy your cogitations (as much as commodiously you may) in some divine matter. Let this be your scope ; let this be the determination of your mind. Labour for this without rest with a quiet and pleasing care. And although every moment (as I may say) you be distracted and stray from your intention, be not dejected ; let not that breed pusillanimity, but be constant, and ever return to what you are resolved. By your indefatigable labour you shall overcome all trouble of difficulty. Nay, in a little while you will find this labour more easy and pleasant ; and being regenerate to the newness of an unknown light, you will begin to taste of the delights laid up for the Saints ; you will not be the same as you were before ; but, being happily changed into another man, and clothed with angelical grace, you will highly esteem what before you despised, and despise what before you highly esteemed. That which before did evilly please you will now displease you ; what before evilly displeased you will now please you : you will promptly and willingly endure what before seemed insufferable. O pleasant metamorphosis ! O change proceeding from the right hand of the Most High. At last, this laudable custom growing into a second nature, and the divine love more perfectly possessing you within, you will not feel any labour ; and as before without labour you did think on filthy, impure, absurd, foolish, vain, and dream like things, so now you will without labour adhere to God and divine things. For, of necessity, the mind must daily reflect on that which the heart dearly loveth.

Woe, woe unto perverse, tepid, and negligent Monks—Monks in name, but not in life—who, contemning the reverence of their state, and violating their vows, are neither ashamed, nor fear to wallow in the dirt and dung of sloth, vanity, and passions. But blessed, yea, ten times triple blessed, are those Monks and Religious men who, albeit they are of little estimation and imperfect, do, notwithstanding, with might and main aspire and tend to perfection; for they are certainly the adopted sons of God, whom our pious Saviour doth comfort, saying, Fear not little flock, for it hath pleased your Father to give you a Kingdom. They may surely expect death, although they are yet but in the beginning of their holy purpose. Because it shall be precious in the sight of our Lord, surely may they expect death; and yet not death, but the sleep of peace, the period of death and the passage from death to life.

What say you, Brother? Are you yet in doubt? Do you yet stagger? Take courage, I pray you, and being emboldened through so great a confidence in

our Lord's goodness, going on the way of salvation
without a fear, preparing your soul against temptations. Let no manner of difficulty affright you. In
all adversity which you happen to endure, either at
home or abroad, say gratefully the will of our Lord
be done. Although you must sweat much and long,
and wrestle strongly before you can overcome and
supplant the old man, let not that trouble you ;
consider not the labour, but the fruit of the labour.
Believe me, the supernal piety will be present at your
labours, and will still most lovingly succour you, will
comfort you when you fear, will confirm you when
you stagger, will defend you being assailed, will
uphold you when you slip, will comfort you in your
sorrow and will now and then infuse the most precious
ointment of internal sweetness into you. If you
persevere, the force of temptations must of necessity
yield to the force of divine love ; temptations and
tribulations will no more be grievous and bitter
to you, but light and sweet. Then shall you see all
good, and shall find a paradise even in this life. This,
I say, will come to pass if you persevere and be not
of the number of them that begin well, but, being
deluded by the allurements of Satan, or wearied with

the troubles of temptations and labours, do afterwards
lightly leave their good purposes. They will not be
pressed with the weight of tribulation, and, therefore,
in time of affliction are scandalized in our Lord, and
going back from Him, do, as it were, seem to say:
This saying is hard, and who can bear it ?

They build not on the firm rock, but on the
unstable sand ; and, therefore, their buildings do
easily fall down at every puff of wind and pushes of
the floods. And would to God they would consider
their ruins, and not so give over, but make haste to
renew the decayed building, no more laying their
foundations upon the sands, but committing them to
the firmness of the rock. Dear Brother, if (which God
forbid) your building be fallen, renew your overthrown
work, and build again more happily than you did
before. If it fall twice, or ten, or a hundred, yea,
a thousand times, or more, repair it as often as it
falleth.   Never despair of God's mercy ; for the
innumerable multitude of horrible and hideous sins
doth not make God so implacably angry with us as
desperation alone ; for he that despaireth of forgiveness denieth the mercy and omnipotency of God and
.blasphemeth against the Holy Ghost   We cannot be

so ready to sin as our Lord is to pardon, if we abuse
not His patience ; that is, if we will truly and in time
do penance. Thus ought every Christian to think.
But, lest prolixity make my treatise displeasing, I
think it best for me to withdraw my pen, and to stop
the course of my begun navigation. In the mean-
while we take down our sails, it will not be amiss
briefly to touch what you ought to do at every day's
end.

Every day, therefore, before you go to bed,
seriously, but without inordinate discipline of mind,
consider in what you have that day offended, and
ask pardon of our most merciful God, purposing
thenceforth to live better, and more carefully to avoid
all vice. Then pray that He will vouchsafe to keep
you that night from all pollution, both of body and
mind, commending to Him and to His sacred Mother
and your holy Angel your soul and body to be
guarded and kept. Being gone to bed, arm yourself with the sign of our Lord's Cross, and having
honestly and chastely composed your body, sigh to
your Beloved, thinking upon some good thing until
sleep gently seize on you ; which, if it be over deep
and rather a burthen than a refreshing to your body ;

if, likewise, by frail illusions it procure or produce anything savouring of dishonesty, be not overmuch grieved thereat, but humbly sigh before our Lord, and with humble prayers beseech Him to grant you sobriety of diet and senses, to which sobriety of sleep and purity of body are commonly companions.

This is all, dear Brother, that I have to send you. You desired a mirror or looking-glass; see whether you have received one. If I have any way satisfied your desire, God be praised; if not, howsoever, God be praised. I have given you what our Lord hath given me; but, be they better or worse, I desire you sometimes to read them over. Fare you well, and pray for me.

FINIS.

BOOKS

PUBLISHED AND SOLD BY

C. J. STEWART,

11 KING WILLIAM STREET, WEST STRAND, LONDON.

Guicciardini Opere Inedite.

OPERE INEDITE DI FR. GUICCIARDINI,

ILLUSTRATE DA G. CANESTRINI.

Firenze, 1857-67. 10 *vols. 8vo, price* 4*l.* 4*s.*

The series of unpublished writings of the great Italian Historian is now completed; and as C. J. STEWART has been appointed by Count P. GUICCIARDINI the Sole Agent in this Country, he is enabled to offer them at £4. 4s., the equivalent of the Continental price 105 fr.

"In rescuing its contents [the collection of Guicciardini's unpublished works] from the repositories of their family archives, the Counts Guicciardini have not merely raised a memorial to their illustrious ancestor, but have likewise furnished a valuable contribution to better knowledge of a most important section of the sixteenth century. The greater portion of these volumes is made up of F. Guicciardini's correspondence, stretching over years of stormy events with which, from his official position, he had much to do . . . In addition to this voluminous correspondence, there are autobiographical sketches, and a series of reflective writings, some of them mere memoranda, but others elaborate disquisitions, which, as a whole, furnish the fullest material to be found anywhere for insight into the workings of a mind that may fairly be considered typical of a class not easily fathomable,—the Italian statesman of the sixteenth century . . . To the last Guicciardini retained unblunted intellectual appreciation for noble aims, though in the atmosphere of a most jealous and suspicious tyranny, he dared to indulge this only in the solitude of his study, where he would relieve pent-up feelings by effusions on paper no living eye but his own was meant to see. After the lapse of three centuries, these ejaculations in writing have been recovered, and like light-shafts sunk into the shrouded depths of nature, they now expose to our gaze the painful heavings and volcanic quickenings that lay unquietly beneath a surface of velvet smoothness."—*Edinburgh Review*, July, 1869; where many other points of equal interest are thrown up.

"The collection of Guicciardini's unpublished papers, which has been given to the world by his family is one of great value and interest."—See *Saturday Review*, Feb. 13, and March 13, 1869.

See also *Quarterly Review*, Oct. 1871.

Miſſale ad uſum Eccleſiæ Sarum.

PARS PRIMA, TEMPORALE.

8vo, *sewed, price* 12s.

PARS SECUNDA, COMMUNE SANCTORUM, MISSÆ VOTIVÆ, ETC.

8vo, *sewed, price* 6s.

☞ The Last and Concluding Part is in preparation.

"The 'Use' or Custom of Sarum derives its origin from Osmond, Bishop of that See in A.D. 1078, and Chancellor of England. . . . We are informed he built a new cathedral; collected together clergy, distinguished as well for learning as for a knowledge of chanting; and composed a book for the regulation of ecclesiastical offices, which was entitled the 'Custom' book. The substance of this was probably incorporated into the *Missal* and other ritual books of Sarum, and ere long almost the whole of England, Wales, and Ireland, adopted it." *Palmer's Origines Liturgicæ.*

"There can be no doubt that this volume will form an epoch in the science of Ecclesiology. When we remember how difficult a thing it was to procure any copy of the Sarum Missal, at what price the worst had to be purchased, how the increased study of the book augmented the cost by which it was to be obtained, it would have been a boon to English Churchmen, the value of which no words could express, to have their own original service book, to have that most precious work of S. Osmond, brought within the reach of the poorest scholar. But, when in addition to this, the Sarum Missal is presented to us with all its various readings, culled from a variety of editions, which we shall hereafter particularise, so that we now have in our hands what of necessity will hereafter be esteemed *the* classical edition of our national Liturgy, we know not how we can return sufficient thanks to the promoter and principal editor of this publication . . . . We know of no equal literary gift which has been bestowed upon the Church, the chief Office-book of which has here been re-edited, from the publication of the First Book of Edward VI. till the present time." *Christian Remembrancer.*

BY THE REV. W. J. BLEW.

On the Proposed New Lectionary [criticising it and suggesting other alterations]. 8vo, *sewed,* 2s.

The Crisis of Common Prayer, a Letter; also the Order for Matins and Even Song, with Morning and Evening Prayer. 8vo, *sewed,* 2s.

The Daily Service divided into Matins and Even Song, and Morning and Evening Prayer: with Preface and Introduction. Oblong 16mo, *cloth,* 2s. or 20s. per doz.

This is a practical plan of abridging the Service by division, without alteration of the present Book of C. P.

The Common Prayer in Latin, a Letter with a Postscript on the C. P. in Greek. 8vo, *sewed,* 2s.

This advocates the use of the Latin C. P., and points out those in prior editions upon which it should be formed.

OPERE DEL CAVALIERE G. B. DE ROSSI.

ANCIENT CHRISTIAN INSCRIPTIONS.
Folio, *sewed*, 4*l.* 8*s.*

Inscriptiones Chriftianæ
VRBIS ROMÆ SEPTIMO SAECVLO ANTIQVIORES.
EDIDIT IOANNES BAPT. DE ROSSI, ROMANVS
VOLVMEN PRIMVM

ROMÆ EX OFFICINA LIBRARIA PONTIFICIA, AB ANNO MDCCCLVII
AD MDCCCLXI.

"The publications enumerated at the head of these pages (*by De Rossi, Garrucci, L. Blant, and Scognamiglio*) are the first-fruits of an earnest and meritorious effort to bring this important branch of Christian archæology within the sphere of exact scientific inquiry, the chief praise of which is due to the distinguished editor of the '*Inscriptiones Christianæ Urbis Romæ.*' In this truly great work, Cav. de Rossi has adhered with severe impartiality to the true principle of inductive investigation. His present collection is but the first step in the inquiry, and is devoted exclusively to the work of bringing together all the facts and data of the study, of subjecting them in detail to a rigorous critical examination, of distributing them into classes, and of arranging them in chronological order.

"The value of M. de Rossi's work will be best explained by a brief *resumé* of the earlier literature of its subject. . . . M. de Rossi's clear and comprehensive Introduction has made the enquiry easy and even attractive; and though there is no part of the author's own Introductory Essay which will not repay the labour of careful and attentive perusal, we shall sufficiently effect our present purpose by a short outline of this branch of Christian antiquities, such as it existed before the recent movement, of which M. De Rossi may be truly regarded as the centre." *Edinburgh Review*, July 1864

"A great and exhaustive work on Christian Inscriptions." *Quarterly Review.*

CHRISTIAN ARCHÆOLOGY.

Bulletino di Archeologia Criftiana

ANNO I. E II. *Romæ*, 1863–4, 4to, out of print; ANNO III.–VII. 1865–9. price 12*s.*; SERIE SECUNDA, ANNO I.–II. 1870–1, roy. 8vo, price 12*s.* each.

EDITION FRANÇAISE, PUBLIÉE SOUS LA DIRECTION DE L'ABBÉ MARTIGNY, ANNÉE V.–VII. 4to, price 12*s.*; SECONDE SÉRIE, I.–II. roy. 8vo, price 12*s.* each.

The *Bulletino* forms a Supplement or Appendix to both the *Inscriptiones Christianæ* and the *Roma Sotterranea*, and therefore ought to be possessed by every one who has those important works. It may also be considered a chronicle of Christian Archæology of those early periods, keeping the student *au courant* in all present researches and discoveries, not in Italy only, but in France, Spain, Germany, Greece, and even Syria and Africa. It also includes contributions on later mediæval subjects to the twelfth century, illustrates the history of the Arts of Architecture, Sculpture, and Painting, and furnishes helps to clear up obscure points of the geography, history, and controversy of those times.

The work appears periodically, and each number contains one or

Published by C. J. Stewart,

OPERE DEL CAVALIERE G. B. DE ROSSI.

Roman Catacombs.

2 vols. folio, 102 Plates in chromo-lithograph, 6*l.* 7*s.*

La Roma Sotterranea Criſtiana,

DESCRITTA ED ILLUSTRATA DAL

CAVALIERE G. B. DE ROSSI,

Pubblicata par ordine della Santita Papa Pio ix. Roma Cromo-litografia Pontificia.

"A large and learned publication." *Dyer's City of Rome.*

"When we noticed, some time ago, the Cavaliere De Rossi's *Inscriptiones Christianæ Urbis Romæ,* we mentioned that he was engaged upon a new history and description of the Roman Catacombs. Of this great work the first volume now lies before us, and we hasten to give some account of it to those of our readers who are interested in this most curious and important branch of Christian Archæology. Every one who knows anything of the modern literature of the subject, and every one who has visited Rome itself knows that the Cavaliere De Rossi is the highest living authority on all questions about the Catacombs and their contents. And he has never been even suspected of a wish to invent, or to distort facts for a polemical object. So that we believe he may be implicitly trusted in matters which have given occasion before now, in other hands, for much angry theological controversy. . . . The book is, moreover, a beautiful specimen of typography, and the plans and chromo-lithographs are well executed. Nor is the price (2*l.* 15*s.*) for which the English publisher is able to supply it, at all excessive, for a quarto volume of above four hundred pages, with so many good illustrations. We mention this because we hope no public libraries will be deterred by a fear of its cost from purchasing this remarkable work. The history of the Catacombs ought to be accessible to all students of Christian archæology. It is to be carefully remembered that the antiquities of the primitive Church of Rome are the common heritage of all Christendom. . . .

"We have said enough to show the extraordinary value of this work to all who wish to investigate the arts, and manners, and customs, and ecclesiastical usages of the first ages of Western Christendom.—*Saturday Review.*

"Of the Christian Catacombs, we have now before us the first volume of what we may consider the classic and authoritative work. It bears the name of the Cavaliere de Rossi, and could not bear a name which would so strongly recommend it to every one who takes an interest in this important subject. . . .

"The Cavaliere de Rossi certainly possesses eminent qualifications for his vast and noble task,—indefatigable industry, sagacity, almost intuitive and prophetic, the power of combining minute circumstances, and drawing out grave and important conclusions by a bold induction from mere points and suggestions, from words and letters; a command of the whole wide and somewhat obscure and scattered world of archæology, which nothing escapes."—*Quarterly Review.*

"The first volume of the new 'Roma Sotterranea' gives us, in addition to the literary history of the subject, a general history of the Catacombs to the time of their final abandonment, and a detailed and special account of that portion of the cemetery of Callixtus which is known as the crypts of S. Lucina. Both parts contain matter of remarkable interest. . . .

"Such a history must ever be eloquent to the heart while Christianity is a living faith. Yet it is but the frame-work, as it were, of treasures yet more prized. If the very story of the Catacombs tells us so much, what ought we not to be able to learn from their inscriptions, their sculpture, their paintings, from their relics that are deposited in their tombs? On these, indeed, volumes upon volumes have been written; we will yet be bold to express our conviction that our knowledge of them is in its very infancy. . . . Here then is a great work to be done; that it will be accomplished before long we see an earnest in the noble volumes already published by De Rossi."—*Christian Remembrancer.*

Imagines Selectæ Deiparæ Virginis, in coemeteriis subterraneis udo depictæ.

GREEK CHURCH.

LITURGIES, IN GREEK.

ANTHOLOGION. Folio, £1.
APOSTOLOS. Roy. 8vo, 6s.
*EIRMOLOGION. 12mo, 4s.
EVANGELION. Folio, 18s.
EUCHOLOGION. 4to, 12s.
*HAGIASMATRION. 12mo, 4s.
HOROLOGION. 4to, 11s.
LEITURGIA. 8vo, 4s.
MENAIA. 12 vols. folio, £4 14s. 6d.
*OCTOECHOS. 12mo, 3s.
PARACLETIKE. Folio, 17s.
PENTACOSTARION. Folio, 10s. 6d.
PSALTERION. 8vo, 4s. 6d.
*SYLLETURGICA. 12mo, 2s.
SYNOPSIS. 18mo, 4s.
TRIODION. Folio, 18s.

With the exception of those with a *, which are stitched only, all the others are in the regular Greek Ecclesiastical binding.

SETS, viz. 17 vols. in folio, 2 in 4to, 3 in 8vo, and 5 in 12mo, are offered at £10 10s.

PANTHEKTE hiera ekklesiastike ton Orthodoxon Christianon. *Athens*, 1860. Vols. 1–5, 8vo, *sewed*, £2 10s.

These are all the vols. which have yet appeared, but another, or perhaps two more, which will complete the work, are in preparation.

ECCLESIASTICAL LAW.

SYNTAGMA KANONUM Hier. Synodon. *Athens*, 1852-9. 6 vols. 8vo, *sewed*, £2 2s.

PEDALION tes mias hagias katholikes kai Apostolikes ton orthodoxon ekklesias. *Zante*, 1864. Imp. 8vo, *sewed*, £1 10s.

Published by C. J. Stewart,

FAC-SIMILE BLOCK-BOOKS.

GESCHIEDENIS VAN HER HEYLIGHE CRUYS

OR,

Hiſtory of the Holy Croſs.

64 *Woodcuts on 33 leaves,*

REPRODUCED IN FACSIMILE FROM THE ORIGINAL EDITION
PRINTED IN 1483, BY J. VELDENER.

TEXT, INTRODUCTION, AND ENGRAVINGS, BY J. PH. BERJEAU.

Fcap. 4to, cloth, 1l. 5s. (fr. 31.25.)

"I may safely promise the reader no small amusement in the description of the volume before us. The materials are equally abundant and interesting, and it will be my own fault if the mode of putting them together be not productive of information as well as of entertainment." *Dr. T. F. Dibdin, in Bibliotheca Spenceriana, on the original at Althorp.*

"Nothing more complete in its way has ever fallen under our notice than this reproduction by Mr. Berjeau." *Saturday Review.*

"The archæologist, the theologian, and the man of letters, will all acknowledge with gratitude the appearance of this unique and beautiful volume. The legend of the Holy Cross may be described as an allegory, parable, or fable, with equal fitness. The truth which it symbolises is familiar to the Christian mind and heart; and the pictorial method of its tradition in unliterary generations is graphic and effective in a high degree.

"The truth itself is this:—That the promise of Redemption was made to our first father, and was the hope which he bore away with him from the gates of Paradise. The promise lived on, from the tradition of Adam till the time of Moses, orally—was recognised by him and the people of Israel in the wilderness—was revived in David, and in Solomon and the prophets—and came to its fulness in the Incarnation. Since then it has been the joy of the faithful, and the offence of the unfaithful in every age, on looking back to the Divine gift of goodness in CHRIST. All this truth is told in *symbol* in the Golden Legend of the Cross. The 'tree' on which our Lord was crucified had been watched, from the creation of the world, with sacred care. The seed from which the future tree would grow was deposited with Adam as he died; and it grew, and was seen by the prophets from time to time; and after the Incarnation it was 'found' and prized by the saints.

"The Latin legend, of which we have here old Dutch, French, and English versions, is said to be originated by Rufinus of Aquila.

"The Introduction and notes are both interesting and learned, and we should be glad to see more on the connexion between this legend, in its numerous forms, with the secret societies of the Middle Ages." *Literary Churchman.*

"M. Berjeau has now put within the reach of every man a book which reproduces a very curious specimen of the earliest art, together with a great deal of really valuable literary information connected with it. The illustrations are in number sixty-four. They are reproduced with the utmost possible care and accuracy from the mediæval original, of which only three copies are known to exist in the world. Of these, besides that from which this book is copied, one is in the King's library at Brussels, the other at the Hague, in the collection of a M. Schinkel . . . .

"Besides the illustrations, however, the volume before us contains an exceedingly curious and interesting relic of mediæval poetry; it is the legendary 'History of the Holy Cross,' in Dutch verses of four lines each engraving. These verses are produced in *fac-simile* below each print; but, besides this, they are printed in clear type, as an Introduction, and with each of them the extract from the Golden Legend, in Latin, referring to the same subject—Caxton's Golden Legend, in English, and the French version from a MS. in the British

11 *King William Street, West Strand, London.*

BLOCK-BOOKS.

Catalogue of Block-Books.

100 *copies printed, which are all numbered, 8vo. price 16s., or 20fr. and only 12 remaining forfeited by Subscribers.*

CATALOGUE ILLUSTRÉ
DES
LIVRES XYLOGRAPHIQUES,
Par J. Ph. BERJEAU.

Ce Catalogue illustré des livres xylographiques ne comprend naturelle-
ment aucune des xylographies détachées, dont le nombre est trop grand
pour que leur description n'exige pas un ouvrage séparé. Nous avons
dans le présent catalogue écarté avec soin tout détail inutile, toute hypo-
thèse de nature à jetter de la confusion dans l'esprit du lecteur. Le
plan suivi dans cette description des block-books est très simple.
Réunir dans le même cadre tous les monuments connus de la xylo-
graphie, publiés sous forme de livres, et mettre l'amateur et le biblio-
thécaire à même de distinguer non seulement les éditions diverses du
même ouvrage, mais aussi de classer dans l'ordre qu'ils doivent occu-
per les feuillets du même livre et de reconnaître au premier coup
d'œil à quel ouvrage appartiennent les feuillets ou même les fragments
que l'on pourrait rencontrer : tel est le desideratum que nous avons
essayé de satisfaire. Nous avons le regret de n'avoir pu décrire qu'im-
parfaitement quelques unes des raretés qui se trouvent à l'état unique
dans certaines collections du continent ; mais, la plupart des monuments sur lesquels des renseignemens complets nous ont manqué
n'ont qu'une importance secondaire.
Il n'existe aucun autre Catalogue complet des livres xylographiques
connus jusqu'à ce jour, aucun recueil bibliographique où l'on puisse en
un instant trouver, sur ces livres si intéressants et si rares, les ren-
seignements que l'on désire.

BIBLIOGRAPHY OF THE SPECULUM HUMANÆ SALVATIONIS.
Eſſai Bibliographique ſur le Speculum Humanæ Salvationis :
INDIQUANT
LE PASSAGE DE LA XYLOGRAPHIE À LA TYPOGRAPHIE.
Par J. P. BERJEAU.

72 *pages, with specimen of the Fac-simile, 4to. cloth, price 10s. 6d. (fr. 13.25.)*

The subject-matter of this Essay is divided into four sections or
chapters :—the *first* entering fully into the question of the Author, and
who he was ; the *second* treats of the Engraver ; the *third* of the Printer ;

FAC-SIMILE BLOCK-BOOKS.

Speculum Humanæ Salvationis :

LE PLUS ANCIEN MONUMENT DE LA XYLOGRAPHIE ET DE LA TYPOGRAPHIE REUNIES.

(63 *ff.*) REPRODUIT EN FAC-SIMILE, AVEC INTRODUCTION HISTORIQUE ET BIBLIOGRAPHIQUE PAR J. PH. BERJEAU.

Only 155 Copies printed.

Folio, cloth, price 4l. 4s. (105 *fr.*) *; mor. old style, 5l. 15s. 6d.* (*fr.* 144.50.)

THE original block-book is supposed to have been printed about 1435, and is of the utmost rarity, the British Museum possessing only one copy. The Fac-simile, which is printed on paper of precisely the same tint and texture as the original, occupies 63 leaves in double columns, with 116 distinct designs ; and a reproduction of the Text in common type is added, so that modern readers may peruse it without difficulty.

The *Speculum* "is simply a pictorial Scripture History, composed exactly on the principle that the stained-glass windows, altar triptychs, and illuminated office-books of the period, pretty uniformly exhibit ; that is to say, a picture of a certain subject from the Old or the New Testament is given, with a more or less brief account, in black letter underneath it, of the personages or scenes intended. The engravings are executed in a very fair style ; indeed, both the drawing and the cutting are wonderful for the age, but the type is not very legible, and is made less so by the many contractions and many barbarisms of the Latinity. Each page has a double subject, under a low, four-centred Gothic arch, resting on a column of what we should call 'perpendicular' or 'third-pointed' details. As regards the drawing, we hold it to be, though rude, very artistic. There is a decided character and an expression in the figures that are almost worthy of Albert Durer. Nothing is feeble, though much is quaint. The draperies are simple and effective, and there is no crowding of figures, but a judicious grouping of from two to five personages in each, with backgrounds of trees, hills, or houses, as in the paintings of the early masters. . . .

"From the learned Introduction which M. Berjeau has prefixed to his fac-simile reproduction, we perceive the importance that necessarily attaches to the present block-book above its two predecessors, and indeed all others, in the fact that it offers the earliest known example of block-printing and printing from moveable type in one and the same volume. . . . The author of the *Speculum* can never be charged with that grossness of language and immoral imagery which are a stain upon many of the theological works of the middle ages." *Literary Gazette.*

"There are several aspects in which a book like this may be viewed. We may consider it as a fac-simile, and admire the perfection of modern art, by which the productions of other ages are imitated with extraordinary accuracy. . . . It is very interesting as an example of the state of wood-engraving some four hundred and thirty years ago. . . . It also indicates that religious teaching was not altogether based on the Bible. For not only are the subjects drawn from the Old and New Testaments and the Apocrypha, but there are a few from other sources. . . . It is remarkable as a specimen of block-printing, and perhaps even more so as combining at the same time the most ancient example of type-printing now extant. Part of it, and of course every illustration, is from wood-blocks, but part of it is printed with moveable type. During its execution the wood-engraver was superseded by the type-founder, and that which was begun as a block-book ended as letter-press. The bibliography of the subject is ably handled by the editor in a copious introduction. . . . Much very interesting matter is contained in this introduction, and it is a valuable contribution to the early history of the art of printing.*

"It is worthy of notice that the ink of the plates and the whole portion printed from the wooden blocks is truly called 'a brown pale and thin ink ; whereas the ink used with the metallic type is of a beautiful and rich black.' These differences, and all other peculiarities of the original copy, have been produced with rare fidelity and success. And as a work of art, therefore, and as a literary monument of a less privileged age, we heartily commend the volume, and have much pleasure in calling to it the attention of our readers. Neither labour, skill, nor money, have been spared in its production.

"Altogether, we know of no book of the kind which the true lover of curious books would prefer to possess, for next to the original he must covet such a fac-simile as this. It is true the sum of four guineas is a high price to pay, but not too much by a farthing for such a work of Art. Its value for the purposes of study and comparison will be evident at a glance to the bibliographer ; upon these points, however, it is unnecessary to enlarge ; and we shall be surprised if any of the one hundred and fifty-five copies, to which the

www.ingramcontent.com/pod-product-compliance
Lightning Source LLC
Chambersburg PA
CBHW020759020726
47495CB00008B/2511